When October Ends

JM Lee

The Novus Proprius Chronicles

Copyright © 2013 JM Lee

All rights reserved.

ISBN-10: 1493708856

ISBN-13: 978-1493708857

CHAPTERS

Prologue.................................5

Chapter 1..............................17

Chapter 2..............................29

Chapter 3..............................41

Chapter 4..............................51

Chapter 5..............................65

Chapter 6..............................79

Chapter 7..............................97

Chapter 8.............................111

Chapter 9.............................121

Chapter 10............................145

Chapter 11............................161

Chapter 12............................191

Chapter 13............................219

Chapter 14............................227

Chapter 15............................247

Chapter 16............................257

CHAPTERS (Continued)

Chapter 17..............................263

Chapter 18..............................269

Chapter 19..............................275

Chapter 20..............................291

Chapter 21..............................327

Chapter 22..............................339

Epilogue...............................347

Prologue

Dear Diary, June 1, 2001

Today was torture. We had to have school on a Saturday because of too many snow days. The weather has been really weird lately. I mean, it is usually piping hot during this time of year for Virginia. But no, we have snow. They have warmer weather in Alaska! Now that is amazing.

It was so weird today. In the middle of class, I heard this lady singing opera. It was annoying me so I asked the teacher if we could ask whoever was singing to stop. But as it turns out, no one was singing! Or at least, I was the only one who could hear it. How is that possible? Now everyone thinks that I'm crazy.

Later some girl named Ember talked to me and said that I wasn't the only one who had heard it. She said she hears it all the time. She also said the singer was a ghost but I don't believe in that sort of stuff.

Last night, I dreamed the strangest thing. I was walking and then I heard a creepy voice whispering in my ear, "Sylvia? Sylvia? Where are you Sylvia?!" The voice was calling to me, but I couldn't tell where it was coming from.

Then, I woke up. When I finally fell back asleep I dreamed the same thing only this time it was calling to someone else. Then it said, "When October ends, you will be the first to die!"

Sylvia Lewis

Dear Diary, June 2, 2001

We had to go to school again today. It stopped snowing, but now we have tornado warnings across the country! The weather is really starting to creep me out. Not only that, but my dogs have been acting weird, too. I mean, our Maltese Katie died because she wouldn't eat or drink anything. All she would do was try and get out of the house and run away. Eventually she just ran out of energy and died.

I still can't believe she's gone. I miss her so much. I've had her since I was a baby and I can't imagine life without her. The house is so quiet I can barely stand it. I just hope whatever craziness got inside her head doesn't get to our other two dogs.

I had the same dream last night, only this time there were more voices. Katie was there too, along with some creepy giant butterfly thing. The weirdest thing about the butterfly creature was that I thought I recognized it.

In the dream, they were talking, but I don't think to me. They kept calling to someone with a very strange and unusual name. It kind of sounded like a female version of the name Adam. Sort of like "Adam-ey." I'm not sure, but I know it was definitely different.

So, the voices said the same thing, "When October ends, you will be the first to die." I'm starting to worry that something is happening. Something abnormal. You know, out of the ordinary. I just hope it doesn't have anything to do with what happened at school and to Katie. I can't take losing another pet, much less hearing ghosts sing at school.

Sylvia Lewis

Dear Diary, June 3, 2001

Man. Eight days of school. When will this torture end? I can't take it anymore, especially with the opera. I have the song she sings stuck in my head. I heard it during Math today. There was the opera followed by screaming. Then there was this evil, manic laughter that followed. I thought I was going to have a heart attack!

You know, that Ember girl is weirder then I thought. Today she was ranting and raving about her "paranormal powers" and how she can see ghosts. Then, she randomly asked me if I wanted to spend the night. I didn't want to seem rude and kind of did want to see what she was like at home so I said, "Sure." We are having a sleepover tomorrow and on a school night too! That's the best part.

Of course, I had the same dream as I always do. Well, it was a bit different than the usual. This time they were all speaking French. I guess the French classes were worth it after all. Anyways, so they said the whole "October" thing again but then they said, "First there will be fire. Then the biggest heartbreak of all." I woke up in a disgusting cold sweat. I hope these dreams end soon.

Sylvia Lewis

Dear Diary, June 4, 2001

Nine days of school now. I feel like my brain is being fried and about to be eaten for dinner. Never will I listen to opera ever again! You know, music doesn't help when your brain is becoming mush.

Ember is asleep right now. I actually had more fun than I thought I would. First we watched this cheesy chick flick and then some rated "R" scary movie. The rated "R" one had a better story to it.

After the movie Ember said, "You promise you won't tell anyone?" I obviously said, "Yes." I mean, who doesn't like secrets? Then she said she was a witch. I really surprised her. She was expecting me to faint or run away or something like that. At first I didn't believe her, but to prove her point, she pulled out a bunch of candles and started chanting. Then out of nowhere appeared a cheesecake. It was amazing! I had never seen anyone do anything like it in my entire life!

I surprised her again. This time she flat out said that most people would run away screaming instead of actually eating the cake. Even though, if you think about it…who could pass up such a good looking cake?

I told her about the dreams I had been having and even asked her if she could do some kind of witch-thing to help me not get them. She said that there was probably a reason why I was getting them. She ended up not doing some kind of witch-thing in the end.

I was a little disappointed. I haven't had a decent night's sleep in such a long time. I guess I was hoping that she could have done something to make everything better. But she didn't. I mean, she's a witch! Something I didn't think existed. Why didn't she help me? What's the point of having powers if you can't use them to help people?

Sylvia Lewis

Dear Diary, June 5, 2001

Though the weather has been acting weird, I never thought it could get this bad. They're saying on the news that we're supposed to get multiple tropical storms in our area for a few days. We're expecting extreme thunderstorms and possible flooding.

School has been canceled because of the storm. I'm happy, but worried that something bad is going to happen. I have this gut feeling that we're in for more than just a storm…but, I'm keeping my fingers crossed that a storm is all that it'll be.

I haven't been dreaming as much, lately. At first, I thought Ember did something after all. Now, I realize that I haven't been dreaming; I've been sleepwalking. In the middle of the night, yesterday, I walked into my parent's room and started yelling that something was wrong and that we were all going to die. They said they tried to wake me up and talk to me, but nothing could calm me down.

Sylvia Lewis

Dear Diary, June 6, 2001

The storms have started. The lightning is so extreme it lights up the sky at night and makes it look like daytime. Everyone is sleeping downstairs because Mom is worried that the neighbor's dead tree in their yard will fall over and hit the house.

I keep sleepwalking. Apparently last night, I was yelling that we were all going to die at the end of October. Then I said that something was terribly wrong. My exact words were, "Something is wrong. We did something to upset them. We're all going to die." Then I whispered, "Take cover."

I don't want to, but my parents are making me take some sleeping pills tonight. They're hoping it will help with my sleeping problems. As much as I don't want to start taking meds, I don't want to upset them anymore. Everyone has been fighting lately. I think it's stress from the storm, the dogs, my sleepwalking, etc. Really, everything in our life right now is chaotic. I just hope everything goes back to normal soon.

Sylvia Lewis

Dear Diary, June 13, 2001

It feels like forever since I've written. The flooding got so bad in our area that we had to evacuate immediately and I didn't have time to grab my diary. Thankfully, we're home now.

Our entire downstairs got flooded, but everything upstairs is fine. Thankfully, that includes my diary. However, all our electronics like our TV and kitchen stuff is ruined. Not to mention our furniture. All our pictures are damaged, too, and all the electronic copies were destroyed when the laptop downstairs got messed up from the water. It feels like a part of our family was washed away with this storm. It's almost like the pictures were the evidence our once happy family. But now that those are gone, everything seems so empty… and lifeless.

When we got home, we couldn't believe our eyes. Most of the water in the house had somehow managed to either drain out or it sunk into our hardwood floors. We'll probably have to completely redo the entire downstairs. The back yard is flooded; there is water up to our knees and our gold fish are swimming around outside of the pond. Trees are fallen everywhere, our yard and the neighbors'. A friend of mine doesn't even have a roof anymore.

Mom got so upset when she saw the damage. She immediately started cleaning when we got home. Dad was so overwhelmed he just went upstairs to lie down, hoping our bedrooms weren't too messed up and our beds still in a good enough condition to sleep in. I guess he was hoping he could go to sleep and then wake up in the morning and everything would be back to normal. In a way, I wish the same.

All I want to do is sleep because I am so incredibly tired. I'm just thankful that my family and I are all safe and home again.

Speaking of sleeping, the dreams are back and the sleepwalking gone. In a way, I'm happy about that. We were sheltered in a school two states over from us during the storm. It would have been embarrassing to sleepwalk with all those people around. But, at the time, that was the least of my worries. We weren't allowed to bring pets, so I had to hope that my dogs wouldn't die in the storm. Thankfully, the pet shelter we left them at wasn't damaged too badly during the storm and they survived.

At the school, there was a little girl named Diliah. She was quite possibly the strangest kid I've ever met. She kept talking about death and war. She was mumbling something in her sleep. I couldn't quite understand her, but I think she said something about the world ending at the end of October. That can't just be a coincidence, right?

Sylvia Lewis

Dear Diary,   **June 14, 2001**

They are calling for a massive storm today; even more massive than the previous one. It is all over the news, and they are warning people to stay inside. Some people are saying it's the end of the world.

The news just said the storm will probably last for the next 48 hours! I wonder if this is the end. I never thought that much about dying. In fact, I never thought about dying at all.

In my mind, I always dreamt of the future. I always saw myself as this happy person with a long life ahead of me. But with everything that's been going on, I've been having so much trouble being the person I used to be. I'm always sad and tired. Since the dreams have started, I've had what feels like a gloomy cloud over my head that makes me worry more than a teenage girl my age should. I should be out having fun with my friends. But instead, I'm worrying about the end of the world. And I can't seem to do anything to change that.

In case it is the end of the world, I would like to take this time to honor my parents for all their hard work and effort that they took in teaching me to do the right thing. I would also like to honor them for not giving up on me. I guess all the hard work they put into making me what I am was just a waste of time. I mean, I don't actually know if the world is going to end. But all the signs seem to be pointing to some kind of an apocalypse. It may not be the end of October, but strange things sure have been happening. I can only hope that I'm wrong, and that everything will be fine by tomorrow.

Sylvia Lewis

Chapter 1

Who knows how many years later…

The school bell had just finished ringing. As I walked through the long deserted hallway, I realized that being late was most definitely not a way to make a good first impression. It was my first day as an 8th grader and though I was thoroughly excited, I was also worried about our subject. In the school newsletters, it said that we were going to learn about an extinct creature called the human. We would also learn about past events and how the human race came to an end—eventually leading us to our species. The werewolf.

As I was walked into my new teacher's room, I was greeted with unwelcoming faces. There weren't too many people in the group; about four or five without counting. While my teacher's face was warm and inviting, there were a few in the group that seemed annoyed by my tardiness.

"Ah, you must be Zaina. Please, take a seat!" She said enthusiastically. I was surprised I wasn't in trouble. It seemed as though I was going to like this teacher, however I would soon discover a whole new side to her.

I hurriedly walked over and sat down next to a girl that

looked as if she were irritated by my presence. I then recognized her as a girl from my pack whose father was the alpha.

"Okay class, now that everyone is here I'll take a moment to introduce myself," she said, standing at the front of the room staring at us all intently. "I'm Ms. Gigi, your assigned Omega. I'm here to take care of you and teach you so if you have any questions or concerns, feel free to ask," she said with a friendly smile, which seemed to turn sour with her next request. "I do, however, ask that you simply call me Gigi. Ms. Gigi sounds too formal and I'd prefer us to think of each other as equals. I'm also not a huge fan of the fact that I'm in such low rank of our pack," she said.

I could tell why the pack had chosen her to be an Omega, those who take care of the younger 'cubs' as they often liked to call us. Most Alphas spoke with a harsh, rigid tone that was unsettling to most younger werewolves. People like Ms. Gigi had what many liked to call a 'silver tongue' which came in handy when trying to tame a group of up to ten or more young, restless cubs.

Looking at Ms. Gigi, who stood at the front of the room still gazing at all of us, I could tell she was your typical slim, tan, blonde haired and blue eyed young adult. The yellow-ish walls of the classroom made her hair seem even more golden.

As we all sat in our somewhat beat up, plastic and metal desks which were left over from the storm many years ago, I noticed the excessive staring Ms. Gigi was doing was her trying to display her dominance though she was only an omega. However, all of us younger werewolves decided it wasn't a good idea to challenge her authority. Everyone reacted differently. Most simply looked down at their desks. I, however, decided to look away and around the room.

I noticed how beat up the room seemed and I could tell it was leftover rubble from the storm we had heard about. You could tell someone had tried to clean it up as well as they could, but there were certain things they just couldn't fix without redoing the entire school. The walls had been recently repainted, yet you could still see random cracks lingering underneath the paint.

"Though you guys are in 8th grade and you probably already know each other from either previous years or from your packs, I'd like to take a moment to introduce ourselves," she said, glancing my way with a friendly, yet firm gaze as if she had her mind set on something extreme.

I gave her a competitive glance as I sat lazily in my chair. I didn't want to speak first, and since she was simply an omega I didn't feel inferior to her. "Let me guess, you want me to start?" I asked, stubbornly.

"Please," she said, crossing her arms over her chest with what sounded like a wolfish sigh.

"Well, my name, as you already know, is Zaina." I nodded; a hint of annoyance in my voice. "Good enough?" I asked, raising the eyebrows I'd carefully trimmed that morning.

It seemed most male wolves allowed themselves to have the bushiest eyebrows, along with extreme facial hair. However, the females who were self-conscious often liked to tame theirs pretty much every day. I and many other girls had no intention of looking like the males of our community.

"More please." She said, slightly pacing around her desk, looking at me as if she thought she were bigger and tougher than her small frame implied. I think I was beginning to cause the hair on her arms to stand up in frustration. The group giggled and snickered a bit but didn't really laugh loud enough for it to count.

"Okay, well, when I was born my parents found out I was a girl, and decided to call me Zaina because they really liked the name." I said sarcastically, managing to avoid the question she was really implying. I always hated talking about myself.

Her lips seemed to tighten together with the slightest bit of anger, though she was trying very hard to smile. "Well, I can see we have our selves a joker here! I was talking about your pastimes. What interests you?"

I sat there and thought for a moment. Ever since I was little, I hated divulging information about myself, and still didn't enjoy it. "Ahhh, okay. Well, I like to read." She looked at me encouragingly, as if sensing my reluctance. "I enjoy reading about horses. They sound like magnificent creatures."

"They are, trust me," Gigi said, with an odd twinkle in her eyes as if she were recalling a beloved memory. "Next!" Gigi called out without waiting for me to ask how she would know.

The girl sitting next to me had naturally curly, shoulder

length, ruby red hair and crystalline eyes. Her gemstone visage made her look like an expensive jewelry box and the forest green blouse she wore brought out the color of her hair even more, giving her a stark, violent beauty. She looked like the type that knew they were beautiful and wouldn't let anyone tell them otherwise.

"Uh, my name is Ruby." *Not surprising*, I thought.

"And I enjoy making clothes." That was rather obvious as well.

I could tell, by looking at her clothes, that they were hand made. They were not poor quality; in fact, they were better than most peoples' clothing. There was just something about the pattern and ruffles of the shirt that made me think she had them specially designed for her.

"Sounds leisurely," Gigi said sarcastically, as if she thought of clothes making as a boring interest to have. "Next?" she said, as if trying to ignore Ruby's uneventful life of trying to make herself all the more beautiful.

Next to Ruby, sat a boy with intense blue-black hair and eyes that looked to be white. He had dark circles under his eyes making him look so much more ghostly. He sat there, practically swimming in his oversized black t-shirt with dark jeans and shoes. He wore all black like many wolves of his pack, though a part of him looked lonelier than all the others. Maybe it was the way his eyes seemed to droop downwards making him look even more depressed than he already did. He also looked like he had been trying to grow his hair out—almost as if to use his hair as a shield from the world.

"My name's Blaze. I enjoyed hunting with my dad." He said with little emotion.

"Enjoyed?" Gigi asked, making an odd face. "Why do you speak in the past tense? Don't you still go hunting with your father?" she asked. I could tell Gigi's continuous questioning was bringing up memories of the past that weren't too pleasant. I hated seeing someone so sad.

"I don't wanna talk about it," he said abruptly. Gigi's eyes widened as if realizing she'd entered into teenage angst territory.

"So," Gigi said, awkwardly looking around the classroom as if to find something else to talk about. "I guess seeing as you're a werewolf, you tend to do that a lot?" Gigi asked. "Hunting I mean," she added for clarification.

Her ignorance made me suspicious from that moment on. Hunting was something werewolves did with a passion. It was almost like a religion to us. Anyone who didn't know that must be of another species.

"Don't we all?" said a ghostly pale girl, three seats over from me. Her tone made me think she was a little annoyed.

"Yes, of course. I just ask because not everyone enjoys hunting," she said with a nervous giggle. Blaze glanced quickly over at the pale girl next to him. Both grinned at each other as if they knew something that I didn't.

Next to go was the girl pale as porcelain. Her eyes were a vivid bloody red in contrast to her milky skin and white hair. I'd never seen a girl so pale with such intense eyes. Her hair was styled in a way that most wolves around here didn't have. It was short and choppy, with many layers; it framed her wide jaw bone just enough to show off the lines of her face.

"My name is Cyprus and I'm an albino—if it's not already obvious. I usually enjoy hunting as well. Blaze and I have actually gone hunting together a couple of times during the winter."

"Usually?" Ruby asked, looking inquisitively at Cyprus.

The girl peered down at her lap, nervously twirling her thumbs, and said, "I feel bad for killing small animals." Her pale skin suddenly lit up with an embarrassing red as if she was ashamed of her feelings. A few of the students in the classroom giggled under their breath as if it wasn't normal to have feelings for the rodents in the woods.

"Oh, don't tease. It's not a bad thing to feel sorry," Ms. Gigi said jokingly. "So Cyprus, are you the only one in your family that is an albino?" Gigi inquired.

The class stared at her in disbelief. She glanced at me as if she were trying to tell me something mentally, but then returned her gaze over to Cyprus.

"Seriously?" Cyprus asked. "As soon as you have one albino in your family, the rest of your family is certain to be one too. Everyone knows that," she said, suspiciously.

Her disbelief was understandable, however. That was also something all werewolves knew. Though it seemed unlikely, I wondered if Gigi was even a werewolf. There was just something odd about her that I couldn't place my finger on. For one, she smelled too clean. Most wolves around here didn't enjoy bathing, yet Ms. Gigi smelled all too much like roses to be normal.

It was a good thing there were only five students in the classroom, or introductions would have taken all day. One thing us wolves weren't well-known for was an abundance of patience. That was another reason they kept the classes so small.

Last but not least was a doe eyed boy with chocolate brown, floppy hair, and mossy green eyes that matched the green shirt he wore. Though his face was rather small, his eyes seemed unusually big, which made it seem like he was staring into your soul. In a way, it made me self-conscious when he looked at me because I felt like he could see right through me.

"Hi, my name is Bob. And I am the bobbiest Bob of all the Bobs in the world." I could already tell he was going to attempt to be the class clown of our small group.

The few of us in the classroom looked around at each other, bewildered. I sat there wondering, *is his name really Bob?* I wasn't sure why, but it didn't seem to be a realistic name to give. Blaze sat, slouched, in his desk, rubbing his head as if he knew 'Bob' was kidding.

He looked at the rest of us buoyantly, and I could tell he really didn't care what we thought of him. "I'm kidding. My name is Bocepheus but I go by Bow. I enjoy telling jokes and watching people make fools out of themselves." *This is going to be an interesting school year,* I thought to myself.

Though Ms. Gigi stood at the front of the class trying to be friendly, I could see that she was a little surprised by Bocepeus' insensitivity. "I'm glad to see we have another joker here," she said sarcastically. "Great. Now that that's all done with, I think we should talk about what we will be learning this year."

It was then that I began to wonder if Ms. Gigi was always so straight forward. In some odd way, it almost seemed like she wanted to rush through things. In retrospect, maybe it was because she felt as though she didn't have enough time. However, school had just begun for us. It also made me wonder what she thought she was going to be late for.

The Novus Proprius Chronicles

Chapter 2

After introductions, the mood seemed to turn sour as Ms. Gigi spoke about this year's curriculum. I could tell by the slight pauses in her speech that the subject was a difficult one for her to grasp. Almost as if she'd experienced the tragedy herself and couldn't handle talking about it to a group of inquisitive students.

"As you all know, we will be learning about an extinct creature," she paused, crossing her arms over her chest as if to shield herself, only to end with a sigh before continuing, "called the human." The painful memories of the subject was almost tangible to me as I sat there, listening, almost feeling pity for the extinct creatures.

"Ms. Gigi, how did they die?" Cyprus interrupted, tilting her head playfully to the side. I also noticed how she peered right into Gigi's eyes, challenging her.

"I will teach you that soon," Ms. Gigi said firmly, keeping constant eye contact with Cyprus to let her know she wasn't intimidating. "Now, back to what I was saying," she said impatiently. "After a few boring days of that, we will be reading some diaries that were found after the major event that caused the humans to become extinct."

"Can we do that first?" Bow asked, sitting in his desk slouched back as if he were extremely bored.

He sat there, gazing out of the window, playing with his papers as if the entire subject of this unknown creature was something that would never come in handy in life. Thinking about it, I didn't think it would either, but it still seemed an interesting enough subject to pay attention to.

"Why?" Gigi asked, looking baffled as she went to go sit down behind her teacher's desk.

"I don't know, maybe because it sounds more interesting," Bow replied, with a look on his face that I didn't quite understand. Then, he said, "I want to know how they lived, these humans of yours you keep talking about. They sound so strange," he finished.

The emphasis he put on the word strange made me wonder how much he knew about these odd creatures I'd never heard about.

"We'll see, Bocepheus," Gigi said with a slight giggle as if she thought his attitude was something to laugh about. Then she asked, "That is how you pronounce it, right?" as if to try and get under his skin.

"No, you pronounce it Bow, because I don't like my full name," he said with great annoyance. By the looks of it, Ms. Gigi had successfully managed to irritate Bow, which was something I thought was very amusing.

"Oh, okay. Sorry, Bow," she said, almost defensively.

"Thank you!" Bow said, throwing him arms in the air as if praising the heavens.

"Now, back to what I was saying," Gigi said, with another awkward, slight giggle. "Later we will learn about some things the werewolf can do that humans can't," she said, getting up from her desk to stand in the front of the room once more.

Why can't she just say we? I thought to myself. It was a little strange to me how she always referred to our kind the way she did. Almost as if she didn't classify herself as one of us.

"Then we will conclude this year with a fun, as fun can be, hunting party!" she said with faked enthusiasm. "I sadly will not be able to join you for that, though some of the other teachers should be," she said, almost sounding relieved.

"Why can't you come?" Cyprus asked suspiciously, once again challenging Ms. Gigi by staring competitively into her eyes.

"Personal reasons," she replied, hastily, as if she had no idea what to use as an excuse. It seemed like Ms. Gigi wasn't too keen on sharing. Then, she looked down at the watch she wasn't wearing and said, "Oh look at the time! Off to lunch with you! Then we can discuss school supplies," she finished, shooing us to the door.

"I'm sorry what?" I asked. Judging by the looks on the other's faces, they were getting ready to ask the same thing.

"Oh never mind, just go eat something already," she said, almost angrily. *More secrets and strange words we've never heard,* I thought to myself. She was acting very suspicious and I didn't like it.

On the way to lunch, I kept asking myself the same question: If Ms. Gigi wasn't a werewolf, what was she? Was she a danger to the school? Or was she as harmless as a fly? Or something more like a deer that was scared of us?

Maybe she was scared that if we found out what she really was, we would want to eat her. We are carnivores after all. But why would she have to pretend to be one of us? Why not just tell us so we had it all behind us, and then there would be no real worries. I guess it depends on what she really was.

As I walked out of the food line, I noticed everyone sitting with their own packs. I would normally go and sit with my own pack, though most weren't here today for some reason. I also couldn't stand most of the wolves in it. Then I looked over and saw Cyprus sitting alone.

I felt bad for her. Albinos were always treated the worst in their packs. They were either treated horribly, or they were shunned completely. Old folklore said that albinos were cursed. They were always considered weaker then their other pack members, yet every albino I'd ever met was perfectly fine.

"Do you mind if I sit here?" I asked cautiously, as I stood in front of her.

"Don't you want to go hang out with your pack?" She asked, looking over at Ruby's gang of dim-witted wolves who practically worshiped the ground she walked on.

"Honestly, I can't stand my pack. And those who I can handle, aren't here because they don't want to deal with alpha-wannabe Ruby and her sidekicks," I said, causing Cyprus to laugh at my insensitivity. "So, can I sit with you?" I asked. It was almost as if Cyprus's excessive evil eye in Ruby's direction had caused her to forget I'd ever asked to sit down.

"Yeah, of course," she said happily. Probably because I was one of the few wolves in this lunch room that was being nice to her and not throwing my steak in her face, or mocking her.

We sat there for a while, not saying much. All that filled the silence was our chomping on stake, which sort of made things awkward. Eventually, I said, "You know, Cyprus is a really pretty name."

"Oh thanks! It was my mom's friend's name actually. She," Cyprus began but seemed to have a hard time finishing. Eventually she managed to continue, "She died right before I was born. My mom said it was a fight that killed her." She looked surprisingly sad.

"Oh, I'm sorry to hear that," I said awkwardly, eating more of my steak.

"It's okay; she didn't have it very easy in life. She was always very sick and weak, so many wolves in our pack thought of it more as a blessing. To many of our pack members, she was considered a burden," she said with an undeniable frown on her face. "Either way, she's in a better place now."

"That's so sad, I'm so sorry to hear that," I said, with a slight pause to stop and take a bite of my food. "Even though she died before you were born, it seems like you knew her better then one might expect," I finished.

She laughed for a moment as if recalling a memory, staring down at her food, almost dreamily. "My mom always tells me that I'm just like her. She said she thinks I might even be the reincarnation of her. She says our personalities are so similar it's almost creepy," she said, still staring down at her food as if she were in trouble.

"That's funny," I said, almost encouragingly. She just looked so sad. "Why does it seem like that's a bad thing?"

"My dad goes crazy when I talk about her," she began, looking around as if to try and spot a pack member in hopes they wouldn't tell her father. "He hated her because she was so weak, and the idea of me being like her bothers him," she paused for a moment. "He doesn't want me to be weak like her because apparently that's an embarrassment."

"That's too bad," I said. "It seems like you and your mom were really fond of her," I said, almost trying to look into her eyes to see if she was even listening to me.

The liveliness that was found in her voice earlier was gone now. Cyprus seemed like a nice, happy girl in class, but now she seemed to be depressed and unfriendly in a way that was unappealing to a person looking for a funny friend to hang out with at lunch.

"Oh, it's alright. My mother and I have gotten used to my father's insensitivity," she said with almost a smirk as if something entertaining was happening. "So anyways," she paused for a moment as if thinking of something to say, "Did you get that weird feeling about Ms. Gigi too?"

Cyprus's attitude and mood was extremely baffling to me. In about two seconds flat she was able to change from gloomy and slightly depressed, to a happy girl ready to talk gossip with close friends.

"Yeah," I began, deciding to go with the flow of things.

"Ya know, some part of me says she's not even one of us. Did you see how she kept getting nervous? And how she kept saying 'the werewolf' instead of just saying us?" I said with my eyes slightly squinted in suspicion.

As we sat there gossiping about the teachers, I was really beginning to worry. Students got kicked out of school for talking about their teachers like this because it was disrespectful to those in a higher rank then them. I definitely did not want to get kicked out.

"Yeah, I noticed that. Plus, she didn't even know how albino genes work," she said, slightly shaking her head as Bocepheus came from his group to sit and gossip with us.

"I know, even my baby sister even knows that! And she's," he began but stopped to pause, rubbing his head. "Is it bad that I don't remember how old my sister is?" he asked, his voice slightly quivering. *Guess he's not very close with his family members*, I thought to myself.

"Did we invite you into this conversation, Bocepheus?" Cyprus asked with mild annoyance. Knowing he hated his full name, she emphasized it even more.

He made a wolfish kind of groan before rubbing his temples and saying, "Do you enjoy torturing me?"

"Yes, I do. It's quite entertaining," she said with a sly,

childish grin.

Once again, Bocepheus groaned before I asked, "So, were you eavesdropping into our conversation or did you just guess what we were talking about?" I looked around nervously to see if any teachers were around.

"Well," he began, shrugging his shoulders. "I was eavesdropping, but only a little," he said innocently. "Hey, guess what!" He exclaimed, most likely to change the subject.

Cyprus and I gave each other a worried glance before saying, "What?" almost in unison.

"The sister whose age I can't remember was trying to learn how to evolve yesterday into her wolf form, and she did it! But then she couldn't un-evolve so I took the time to teach her things like 'sit' and 'roll over.'" He said in amusement. "Does that make me a bad roll model?" he mumbled to himself, looking up into the air.

Suddenly, memories were triggered. I remembered when I first started school. I remembered being in school and learning vocabulary words like 'evolve' which meant to turn into your wolf form and back into human form. I could never understand why they called it that. I also remembered how difficult a skill it was to master. In the beginning, you could be thinking about squirrels or other small animals and you would turn because the wolf in you would suddenly decide it wanted to hunt.

The first half a year of our training was strictly for learning to control your inner wolf. It was said to be the hardest thing for a pup to learn, so the strictest of teachers were assigned to the job.

Next thing I knew, Ruby was sitting at our table gossiping with us as well. "So, if you guys think Ms. Gigi isn't a werewolf, what do you think she is?"

"I don't know, maybe she's some kind of new species that we don't know about," I suggested. I felt like I was a little too excited for the situation. However, thinking of the possibility of different species existing, other then our own, seemed absolutely incredible.

"Zaina, you're so full of it! If Ms. Gigi was some kind of species that we didn't know about, the school wouldn't let her anywhere near us for our safety," Ruby said, causing me to think choice words that weren't appropriate for school.

"But what if they didn't know? Maybe Zaina is right, and

she is something else, and the school doesn't even know. Did you ever think of that?" Blaze said, coming out of his dark corner he sat in to eat lunch. It wasn't until then that I realized he had been sitting at our table the entire time.

"Blaze, we never invited you into this conversation did we?" Ruby said with her finger waving up in the air.

"They never invited you either," Blaze snapped, throwing the rest of his food into the nearest trashcan.

She groaned as she said, "Whatever" and went back to her little posse of sheep who practically worshiped the ground she walked on.

"Thank God 'it's' gone," Blaze said, and for the first time I saw him smile. The sight seemed refreshing compared to his usual depressed visage.

Chapter 3

As lunch came to an end, our little group dissipated as Cyprus and I talked about things we had read. I, of course, talked about nothing but horses simply because that was the only thing I'd ever read about from the old world. Cyprus seemed to have an interest, or should I say obsession, with humans. If there was anything to know about the strange creatures, she knew it.

"Did you know humans didn't live in caves? They lived in these things called houses that usually had more then one floor!" Cyprus said, her eyes lighting up from the subject.

"They did what now?" I asked. Though I couldn't see my face, Cyprus's reaction let me know that my confusion was somehow hysterical.

She began to chuckle and as she told me about the strange living arrangements of our ancestors. "They built something called a house that was made out of either wood or brick," she said, talking slowly so I could retain all the information. Though she was smart, she had a tendency to treat those less intelligent than herself as complete idiots.

"Okay," I began, though I was cut off by Cyprus's rant

about humans.

"Also, their houses weren't rounded on top! They were pointy! Isn't that weird? I can't imagine my cave being twice as tall and pointy. That would just be strange," she rambled, probably thinking of the drawings she'd seen in text books. "You know how we do research for projects and stuff?" she said, her eyes widening in excitement.

"Um, yeah, sure," I said, shrugging. I wasn't quite sure where she was going with this, but I played along as best I could.

"They had this thing called the internet! And they could do their research on this internet place, and apparently it was so much easier and faster then what we have now," she said, getting even more excited as time went on. "Gosh, I can't believe I don't remember what that thing was called," she said disappointedly.

"Are you talking about Google?" Bocepheus asked, as he walked by, probably eavesdropping once again. It seemed like that was one of his strengths.

"Thank you, but no thank you!" Cyprus snapped back, though it seemed like Bocepheus was merely trying to help her out.

He rose to his defense and said "You would never have remembered it anyways," He rolled his eyes, as he began walking away faster.

"Okay, whatever. Bye now," Cyprus said. I couldn't figure out why they seemed to hate each other so much. Though their constant mockery was entertaining, I couldn't figure out why.

She suddenly looked back at me in excitement as if ready to start rambling. However, before she could go off on a tangent again, I said, "Oh look, there's the classroom! Maybe we can talk later a bit more about all these human things."

"Okay," she mumbled, sounding almost depressed. I couldn't figure out what she found so interesting about those creatures. They were so strange and different then us, though at the same time so similar in so many ways.

As we walked into the classroom, a teacher named Mrs. Xena was talking to Gigi, and she didn't seem too happy. I suddenly began to worry that she'd heard us during lunch and was telling Ms. Gigi to straighten us up.

"I'm sorry, but I never said that," Gigi said innocently. She looked like she was about to cry. There were definitely tears in her eyes, but she seemed like the kind of person who would do that just to add dramatic effect.

"We'll see about that," Mrs. Xena said, accusingly. "I mean, Gigi, this is your job! Not mine. I won't keep covering for you. Either tell them, or quit," she finished as she stormed out of the room.

Gigi stood at the front of the room rubbing her head, worriedly. "Please children. Take a seat." You could see the distress in her eyes from across the room.

"What were you two talking about?" I asked, though I could tell I was being a bit too nosey.

"Zaina, you should know by now it's rude to ask grownups what they argue about!" She snapped. My mind went blank as she spoke. Once again, she spoke in strange tongues that were not familiar to me.

"What does 'argue' mean?" Blaze asked, letting me know that I, thankfully, wasn't the only one who didn't know what that word meant.

"Um, arguing means," she paused. "Oh gosh. What have

I gotten myself into?" there was a short pause, then—

"Arguing is when two or more werewolves discuss a subject they are not fond of? Then they usually end up fighting…with words?" She said, causing me to agree with the common blonde stereotype.

"What?" seeing as, I'm sure, all five of us were thinking the same thing, I figured it didn't matter if I asked.

"Um, hum. Well, it is when two or more people disagree about something, and discuss it, I guess." She said, hoping this time she had a better answer.

"Okay?" Ruby said with a slight attitude, thus avoiding direct eye contact with Gigi to try and remain as respectful as possible. "What are school supplies?" Ruby asked stubbornly, forgetting she was trying to be respectful.

"Uh, supplies you use at school?" Gigi said sarcastically, shrugging her shoulders and beginning to pace around the room.

"We kind of figured that much," Blaze said in his usual tone.

"Then why do I need to explain them?" She asked, sitting down on her desk, looking slightly confused.

"Did the humans use school supplies?" Cyprus asked, surprising all of us by the fact that there was something about humans that she didn't already know.

"Yes, they did. In fact, every year before school started, they would get a piece of paper, much like your newsletters, and it would tell them what they needed for the coming year of school," she said, opening up a text book and pretending to get her information from that. However, we could all tell that she and Cyprus had a similar obsession for humans. Sometimes I found it eerie how much they knew about them.

"What kinds of supplies did they need? Like food or something?" Ruby questioned, looking more confused then ever as she played with the books on her desk.

"Well no. They needed something called a pencil. It was a piece of wood that had something called lead in the middle of it that allowed them to write with it," she said shrugging, getting up to pace around the room once more.

"So," Bow looked at Gigi confused. "Was it was magic?" I couldn't help but chuckle under my breath, thinking, *at least Ruby isn't the only brainless one.* Bow glared at me from across the room as he heard my mocking chuckle.

"Um, well no. But I guess if you want to think of it that way you could," she said with a slight chuckle also. "But see the thing is that, back then, werewolves didn't exist. Magic and werewolves were fake. You would have been considered myths back then," Gigi said, seeming to have a little too much fun. It was almost like story time; I couldn't even imagine this crazy world her and Cyprus talked so highly of.

"Why didn't we exist?" Bow asked. He wasn't the only one who couldn't grasp the concept of their own kind not existing. It all seemed insane. It almost felt like Ms. Gigi was lying to us.

"I'm not sure. I guess the werewolf just hadn't evolved enough yet. There were either wolves or people. But never were there cases of werewolves such as you five," she said, smiling at her dazed and confused students.

"Why is it you have trouble talking about humans being extinct, but you can talk about us not being evolved yet?" Blaze asked, grinning wickedly. *And if we didn't exist then, why are we here now?* I questioned myself though I was too nervous to ask it out loud.

"Uh, not sure." She looked nervous again, her pacing beginning to speed up.

Her nervousness seemed to be a clear indicator that she was hiding something from us. I could feel it in my gut the way I could feel danger lurking around a corner during the hunt.

"Okay kids. Time for you guys to go home," she said suddenly, looking almost relieved. "Make sure you bring pencil and paper tomorrow!" Gigi said waving as the bell rang.

"I don't think they sell pencils here," I said as I inched my way to the door. I wonder why she talked so funny. Yes, she was a teacher, but she had such a strange speech pattern that didn't make sense to us younger wolves.

"Oh sorry, ink. That's what I meant!" Gigi said, looking like she was going to smack herself in the face for her mix up of her words.

Our ink was quite interesting. It was made of the syrup from the Jaku flower's nectar. *Whoever came up with a name like that needs a life*, I thought as I continued to walk away.

"Did the humans bring those things to school?" Cyprus

asked, though most of us were already out of the door.

"Um, yes dear. They did." I heard Gigi say to Cyprus as I walked down the hall way to leave the school.

The Novus Proprius Chronicles

Chapter 4

As the old fashioned, hand-rung bell sang its song to let us know it was time to go home, I saw Mrs. Xena and Mr. Tash talking and constantly pointing at Ms. Gigi's room. *I wonder what they were talking about*, I thought. Earlier, when Mrs. Xena and Gigi were talking, if that's what you want to call it, they seemed to be having a pretty important 'argument', as Gigi called it.

I began to wonder who she was supposed to tell something to and what. I wondered if she was supposed to tell the school something. Or, perhaps us? Who knows, Ms. Gigi seemed to be unpredictable. She was one of those people who you couldn't trust because you never knew what they were hiding up their sleeve.

Suddenly, I felt two hands grab my shoulders and begin shaking me as someone growled directly in my ear, scaring me out of my endless OCD thoughts. I looked back and realized it was Cyprus, though before I saw it was her, I let out a high pitch shriek that caused everyone in the hallway to stop and stare.

"Zaina? Why did you just scream?" Mrs. Xena said

sternly from across the hallway, probably remembering how much of a pain I was back in my first year of school.

"Sorry Mrs. Xena," I said, looking down at the ground to seem as respectful as possible.

Mrs. Xena looked over at Mr. Tash and nodded. *Uh-oh, the nod was never good!* I frantically thought.

"You're excused, go home." Mr. Tash said sternly, pointing at the door, signaling not only me, but everyone in the hallway to finally get going and leave.

"He scares me," I whispered to Cyprus. I hoped he hadn't heard me, because phrases such as those were considered disrespectful and could also get you kicked out of school.

"He scared everyone, and he knows it, too," Cyprus said, a little too loud for comfort. Though we were outside of the school now, the teachers still had sharp hearing. I had no plans of getting kicked out of school for something a friend of mine said. "Me and Blaze are going hunting later," Cyprus said, most likely trying to change the subject. "Think you wanna join us?"

"I'll have to make sure my parents are cool with it, but it sounds fun," I said with a smile; hunting was something I was good at and really enjoyed. This was so much more fun then talking about humans. "We're low on food anyways. But," I began, pausing for effect. "I would hate to interrupt something," I said, raising my eyebrows slightly.

"What do you mean?" Cyprus asked, looking dazed. It was almost as if she knew what I was hinting at but simply didn't want to admit it.

"Well I don't know," I said with an almost smug smile. "You two seem pretty comfy," I finished, feeling slightly content somehow. Recognizing things such as Cyprus's and Blaze's future relationship seemed so satisfying.

"What?" She said, her voice raising a tad in alarm. "No! He's like a brother to me. We're just friends—I don't think of him like that!" she said, though her alarm was quite amusing to me.

I began to laugh hysterically because of her reaction and said in between laughs, "It okay, Cyprus, I'm just messing with you! But, you two would make an adorable couple." Her face suddenly turned from alarmed to slightly angry, but I couldn't think of why. *It was only a joke—sort of,* I thought to myself.

"I don't see why this is so funny to you," she said, almost looking hurt. I couldn't figure out why, especially if she said they were simply friends.

"It's okay," I said, attempting to contain my laughter. "It was a joke. I'm just doing what any good friend would do," I said. *Friend*, I thought to myself, *that's a new one*. "It's kind of like you scaring me just now," I said, hitting her shoulder ever so slightly.

"Whatever you say," she said, smiling a tad.

After some extra chit-chat about school and the people inside it who we either didn't like of liked a lot, Cyprus told me where to meet her later to go hunting with her and Blaze. I felt a little excited. I wasn't used to people inviting me to hunt with them. I supposed I was used to being the lone wolf.

I took the long way home, trying to waste time so I wouldn't have to wait to hunt with Cyprus and Blaze. When I stepped through into our cave, I was greeted by the smell of a soft crackling fire that seemed to be begging me to sit by it. I did as it wished as the flames danced high into the air and the smell of smoke filled my lungs.

I walked outside, feeling my chest tighten from the smoke. "Mom?" I called, looking around. I didn't see her so I called out, "Dad?"

As I stepped outside, I saw my mom stalking a small squirrel. She had her long amber tail high in the air, and her dark hazel eyes set on the rodent. I was afraid to interrupt. Many people were extremely aggressive after they'd missed a kill. And if there was one thing my mother was known for, it was that she had a high temper.

I suddenly felt a presence behind me, as I heard my father say, "Honey, don't move." He whispered slow and quiet, making me wonder what the matter was.

"Why not?" I said slowly, beginning to turn around to look at my father.

"We need food, don't we?" he said, emotionless. He was probably hungry, judging by his mood.

"One squirrel isn't enough to feed us all!" I said, a little too loud, causing the squirrel to react and run away. I heard my mother growl, probably out of annoyance, as she lunged for the rodent.

The squirrel squealed at the top of its lungs in agonizing

pain. I was about ten feet away, and could still hear the crunching sensation when my mother snapped the small animal's neck.

My mother shook her head repeatedly to get the rodent out of her mouth before she evolved back to her human form. Then, she said, "That's why we're going to be busy for a while."

I took this as an opportunity to ask for permission to go hunt. "Well, some friends from school are going hunting and they wanted to know if I could come," I said, hoping they were in a good mood. My parents were so much more willing to let me do things when they weren't angry or upset.

"Who are these friends?" my father asked, crossing his arms and looking suspiciously at me.

"Their names are Cyprus and Blaze. You probably know them from their packs," I began, though I could tell he had remembered them. Our pack and Cyprus's pack were rivals for reasons I could never quite figure out. We, technically, weren't supposed to be friends, but that didn't seem to stop us along with many others.

"I don't want you hanging out with those," he began,

but paused.

Before he could say anything offensive, I said, "Dad! It's not always just about a pack and their leaders you have a problem with! Sometimes it's about an individual despite their pack, okay?"

Though I was trying to remain calm, it wasn't quite working out for me. I'd always hated when someone was discriminative towards another wolf because of the pack they came from.

My father was going to say something negative, when my mother cut in and said, "It's fine, just go and bring us back something good." I was glad she ended the conversation before it got out of hand.

"Just make sure albino girl doesn't bite it," my dad snorted. I could never quite figure out why everyone hated Albinos so much.

I was about to turn around and use a few choice words when my mother said, "Go! They're probably waiting for you."

"Whatever," I began. "Bye," I said emotionlessly as I walked away, waving with my back turned to them.

I walked for a long time, pondering many things such as the strange behavior of Ms. Gigi, my father's hatred for Albinos, my mother's patience in human form yet hot headedness in wolf form. I'd always found it so strange to think of the fact that we could morph our entire bodies into an animal and then back into what looked like a human. The thought seemed so unrealistic when learning about our ancestors and the fact that they couldn't do such things.

When I was finally at the forest were Cyprus and I said we were going to meet I couldn't see her, I only saw Blaze leaning on a tree examining a strange looking plant that neither of us had ever seen before. When he noticed me standing next to him, also looking at the plant, he jumped back a little.

"Where's Cyprus?" I asked, still looking at the plant. I wanted to be daring and poke at it, but the last time I did something like that, my skin swelled up and became itchy. Later I found out it was something called "poison ivy", something from the old world. No one knew how it had gotten here.

"She never told me you were coming along," Blaze said rather monotone, though still looking annoyed. He completely ignored my question as he straightened himself up.

"Is it a problem if I do?" I asked, also standing up. The stance he was in made me think he was trying to challenge me.

"No, I guess not," he said, slouching slightly, as if to let me know he was no longer attempting to be some macho man. "It's just dangerous enough with two people, but with three? We could be spotted easily," he said, looking worriedly at the ground, kicking up some grass.

"Spotted?" I asked, looking around worriedly. "By who?" I finished my sentence, looking frantically up at Blaze for some answers.

"You don't know?" he asked, raising an eyebrow, deviously. By now, many had come to know his pack as the pack of tricksters. They were quiet, but they played dangerous games with your head.

"Know what?" I asked, hoping he would finally just tell me what was going on. At this point, he was really starting to creep me out. But then again, Blaze seemed like the kind of guy who would do such things intentionally.

"I've heard rumor about a new species," he began, pausing for dramatic effect. All this running around the answer instead of just spitting it out already was beginning to drive me insane. "The butterflies—they've evolved too. Obviously not into wolves. But into humans. For all you know, any one you see could be a giant, carnivorous, flying beast," he said, smiling for what seemed like the first time ever.

"Butterflies?" I asked, sarcastically, folding my arms across my chest. "I'm pretty sure last time I checked," I pointed over to a normal sized butterfly flying a couple feet away from us and said, "they were just butterflies." I didn't believe him for one second.

"Those kind are," he said, pointing over to the same butterfly. "But apparently, there are people in our community that change into giant butterflies that eat our kind," he finished, still smirking an almost menacing smirk.

"I don't believe you," I said, shaking my head. "Now, when will Cy be here?" I asked, putting all my weight onto one foot.

Suddenly I heard a rustle in the grass behind me. "That might be one of them," Blaze said, sounding terrified in an entirely fake way.

"You're a really bad actor," I told him, though suddenly I felt someone jump onto my back as they attempted to bite at my neck.

My instincts took over as I threw the person off my back and onto the ground. "Geez, Zaina. What was that for?" Cyprus asked, rubbing her neck gingerly. I suddenly felt bad. It always seemed like I somehow ended up hurting my friends.

"Oh my gosh, Cy!" I said, helping her to her feet. "I'm so sorry! I had no idea it was you!"

"It's okay," she paused, popping her back. "I guess I had it coming, huh?" she asked, with a kind of pitiful grin. "It was worth it though," she said laughing.

"Ha-ha, very funny," I said, lightly punching her in the arm. *That probably wasn't a good idea,* I thought to myself.

"So you hurt the poor girl even more?" Blaze said defensively, holding his hand up to Cyprus's arm where I'd slightly hit her again.

"It's okay," she said, smiling at Blaze. I could tell she liked the attention he gave her.

"No it's not, are you okay?" he asked, examining her to

make sure nothing was broken or bleeding.

"I'm fine really," she said, lightly laughing. "We should probably get going though, shouldn't we?" she asked, looking at me.

"Yeah we should. If I take too long my dad will come out here and find me and accuse you of somehow hurting me," I said, looking down at the ground in embarrassment. "Sorry, but my dad really doesn't like that you're an albino." We began walking towards the woods.

"Yeah, most parents don't," she said, looking almost ashamed because of her genetics. "I don't see what's so wrong with us, though. I guess it's the red eyes. They do tend to scared people," she said, staring down at the ground. Blaze put his hand on her back as if to comfort her. I could tell she'd had a lot of problems with her albinism.

"I don't see why, I think they look cool," I said with an encouraging smile.

"Really?" she asked, looking hopeful and happy.

"Yeah!" I said, excitedly. "It makes you unique, because you're not like everyone else," I said, and I could see Blaze and Cy both smile.

"You know, I have white eyes," Blaze said, as if he were trying to impress us both. Cyprus simply laughed at his foolishness.

"Yes Blaze, we know," Cy said, smiling. I could definitely tell there was something there between the two of them.

The Novus Proprius Chronicles

Chapter 5

Though none of us really believed the rumors, we still decided it would probably be safer to be in wolf form. It was the first time I'd seen the two of them in their evolved state, and I couldn't help but marvel at the beauty. Though they were both attractive people in human form, their wolf forms just seemed so much more majestic.

Cyprus had a coat that looked softer then any blanket I'd ever seen. It was a pearly white that almost seemed to shimmer in the sunlight. Her blood red diamonds for eyes pierced everything she looked at as she stalked through the woods. Her small snout was accompanied by small petite teeth, however they looked like tiny little needles that could hurt more then any other fang you'd see around here. Everyone always said the smaller the teeth, the bigger the pain.

Blaze was a whole different story. His coat was a rough, jet black that looked dry and rigid, much like his personality. His coat might not have been the nicest, but his glazed, white eyes looked like tiny piles of snow amidst a field of dark, dead grass. Though he didn't seem to have large claws or teeth, he had a menacing presence; one you wouldn't want to mess with if you intended to walk away unharmed.

He might not have had many natural weapons, though he had tough rigid muscle that made him look like he could handle a fight or two.

Much like many of the other wolves of my pack, I was smaller then Cy and Blaze. A lot of wolves liked to joke that the reason my pack didn't like other packs was because of our unusual size. Though we were still quite large, for some reason we were simply smaller in size. While Blaze's pack was full of young, fit wolves with bulging muscles most of the time, my pack was filled with wolves that were long and lean. My pack members and I were runners; we could outrun any wolf that tried to beat us, but we were often considered weaker.

I looked at Cy and Blaze's coats, and felt slightly jealous. Not only were they both stronger then I, they were more beautiful. My coat was a mix between soft and rough, but it was short. Due to my sufficient number of freckles, my auburn colored coat also had dark brown dots here and there. My eyes were a little greener in wolf form then they were in human form, though there didn't seem to be anything special about me.

I ignored my slight jealousy as we continued to walk

through the woods. After about an hour of walking, we stopped to think. We couldn't seem to find any deer. The best alternative was to try and come up with a plan to weed them out.

As we stood there, thinking of a plan, we heard what sounded like a storm coming. All we could hear was wind coming hard and coming fast. Suddenly, we saw a shadow fly over our heads. *I don't think that's a storm*, I thought frantically, also thinking about what Blaze had told me.

I evolved back into human form to talk to the others frantically. "Guys, what was that?" I said nervously, as Blaze and Cyprus evolved also.

"I have no idea," Cy said, fearfully. The only one who seemed to be staying calm was Blaze.

"That shadow was huge! It looked bigger then all three of us," I said, looking worriedly at the sky.

"Trust me," Blaze began. "Way bigger," he finished, seeming a little too calm for comfort.

"How do you know?" Cyprus asked, a little attitude, a little curiosity mixed into her voice. As both of us looked over to where Blaze was staring, we suddenly realized how he knew.

Cyprus, Blaze, and I all stood there and gawked at the strange creature in front of us, not knowing if it was safe to move or not. Standing just a few feet away was something so beautiful and menacing at the same time, it almost couldn't be described. *The rumors are most definitely true,* I thought to myself. Yes, it was a butterfly, though there were some features to it that I didn't think normal sized butterflies had.

Its face was long and thin, though the area where the huge bug eyes were located was scrunched in like a Pug's. The body was long and thin, covered in straw-like, midnight black hairs—it looked rather rough, maybe even sharp. The wings were much like a monarch's wings, though the tips fanned out into sharp points like knives. The wings were mostly black, with a few burgundy accents. The sharp blades at the end were reddish-purple along with three dots in the center of each wing. It was definitely a frightening thing to witness, though it still seemed beautiful if you ignored the scrunched up face and awkwardly hairy butterfly legs.

"Blaze!" I yelled, and he looked over at me confused. "You jinxed us!" I said, frustration and panic in my voice.

"How did I do that?" he asked innocently, for the first time since I'd known him. This definitely wasn't some joke his pack was playing on us. The butterflies were real.

The beast in front of us continued to come towards us. Confused at what was going on and scared of what might happen, I continued to yell at Blaze.

"*You* were the one who said that the butterflies had evolved into carnivorous giants!" I said, looking up at the monster as it came closer and closer to us. "Let's just hope they're not, well," I started, not wanting to finish my sentence.

"Carnivorous?" the thing asked, shaking its wings a little. Its voice was rather high pitch; higher then I had expected at least.

Cyprus began to back away slowly. Then she yelled, "It talks?"

"Wow, just wow," it said, looking somehow astonished at Cy, though it was kind of hard to tell in its butterfly form. "And anyway, 'it' has a name!" the thing finished mockingly.

"Okay?" I said, looking at my two friends. Why was this thing being friendly? "Then what is it?" I asked shyly, looking down at the ground.

Its face seemed to lighten up as it said, "Tio," quite simply.

"Um, okay Tio. Are you—carnivorous?" I said slowly, looking around to make sure there weren't more.

"Yes," Tio said, with what seemed like an attitude—almost like it expected us to already know everything about it. *My worst fear, come to life,* I thought to myself frantically, *a carnivorous butterfly! How on earth do you find a giant, carnivorous butterfly?*

"Were we," Cy began, "disturbing you?" she finished cautiously, looking around as if planning an attempt to escape.

"Yes, in fact, I was just hunting." Tio said, merrily. We all looked at each other. This thing, Tio, it was bigger than all three of us! If we made it mad, it could eat us in, probably, one big gulp.

"Oh!" Blaze said, though it sounded more like a gasp. "Well, we'll just leave you to your hunting then. I guess we'll be going," he said frantically, looking at Cy and me anxiously.

"What? No, please stay," Tio said, smirking. It seemed to be enjoying this all too much.

"Please don't eat us!" Cy pleaded, though I couldn't figure out why she wanted to put that idea into the beast's head.

"I have no intention of eating you," it said, laughing hysterically. "We're all hunters! We should be friends. Maybe we can help each other out. Besides," it began, "I've tried wolf and it's not as good as everyone says it is—too chewy," it finished, knowing it was scaring us all half to death.

"W-what?" Cy asked, looking around once again.

Tio suddenly busted into another fit of hysterical laughter and said, "I'm just kidding! But, you should've seen your faces. It was priceless." It continued to laugh, though we didn't seem to find it very funny.

"Anyway," I said, trying to change the subject because the current one was making me extremely uncomfortable. "Do you know where all the deer are? We can't seem to find any," I said, hoping that while flying, Tio had seen some.

"Just because I can fly, doesn't mean I can see everything," it said, with a surprising amount of attitude for a butterfly, something I didn't think could talk.

"Sorry, I was just curious," I said, looking awkwardly away from Tio. *It's like she knew what I was thinking,* I thought to myself.

Then, suddenly, I heard some rustling behind us. Then a twig snapped. My heart stopped, and the blood stopped flowing for a moment, as my head began to heat up in fear.

The thoughts running through my head were terrifying. Did Tio double-cross us? Did she trick us into believing she was not going to hurt us, or was she just as surprised and scared as us?

I slowly turned around, while Cy and Blaze still stood there in fear, not knowing what to do. Behind us, were two more butterflies who looked almost identical to Tio. And judging by the looks on their faces, our faces were extremely amusing.

Once Cy realized what was going on and who was behind us, she let out a heart-stopping shriek and caused my blood to begin flowing again. "They always scream," one of them said, shaking its head.

"Why did you have to step on a twig?" One of them

said, punching the other in the wing.

The other butterfly ignored the question and continued to rant, saying "Why is it that every time we try to scare somebody, and then one of us steps on a branch or something, they scream, even though we didn't even get the chance to scare them? I mean, it happens every time!" it said, sounding annoyed, as Cy continued to scream.

Tio just sat there rubbing her head with the side of her wing. There were too many identical butterflies around us that I could barely tell who was talking or even how to differentiate them. The only thing I could tell was that Tio was most likely a girl because she was smaller in size and had a high pitch voice.

"Did you ever think that they might be scared of your face?" the other one said. This was the most emotion and attitude I'd seen a butterfly project.

"Hey, what's that supposed to mean?" he said, looking offended.

"Well, your face has never been that flattering to look at! I'm almost scared to look at you because you're so ugly," he said, examining the other butterfly head to toe. My guess was that he must have been the younger brother of the other one. One thing was certain, however, and that was that they were definitely related somehow.

When she noticed the two arguing with each other, she stopped screaming, stepped back in confusion and said, "Um, I'm confused. Who are you?" She pointed at the both of them and looked back at Tio as if they were long lost friends.

"I'm sorry, these are my annoying brothers, Hazere," she said as the one who called the other one ugly raised his wing, "and Twig," The supposedly ugly one raised his wing. Really, they all looked the same to me.

"And who would you be?" Hazere said. Though the question was intended for the three of us, I couldn't help but notice his gaze rested on Cyprus.

"Cyprus" she said shyly, raising her hand and looking down at the ground, blushing. *Odd,* I thought. She didn't blush that much when she introduced herself in class today.

"My name's Zaina," I said, looking at the three butterflies around me, nervously. I still didn't trust them. For a moment, I noticed Twig staring at me oddly, almost as if he recognized me somehow.

As usual, Blaze said his name simply and emotionlessly. My guess was that he was trying to look tough and probably cool, though it didn't seem to be working out for him.

"I go by Haze," said Hazere matter-of-factly. "It's just easier," he finished, shrugging his butterfly shoulders.

Tio looked at me and said, "Why is it you werewolves have such fancy names?" It was almost as if she were jealous.

"I don't know," I said, suddenly feeling self-conscious about my name. I'd never thought of it as fancy.

"Just wait till you hear some other names!" Blaze said, rolling his eyes.

"Why don't you surprise me?" she said, looking at all three of us straight into the eyes. Was this a normal thing for them? Because it seemed like they were all doing it.

"Well, there's Mrs. Xena, Mr. Tash, Mrs. Heyssdeff. Names like that," Cy said, her inner nerd once again being exposed. I noticed that ever time Haze looked at Cyprus she seemed to stumble on her words which seemed adorable to me, but utterly annoying to Blaze.

"There's also Ruby, and some really annoying kid named Bocepheus, but he goes by Bow," I replied. "Those are the other kids in our class," I finished, looking away from Twig's intense stair.

"Bocepheus?" Twig exclaimed with an odd laugh. "Impressive, that's even more odd then Zaina," he said, mockingly, as if trying to get under my skin.

"Hey! What's that supposed to mean? My name's not odd! It's just," I babbled.

"Different?" He raised an eyebrow, staring directly into my eyes, causing me to become uneasy; Tio had looked away from me and was staring into Blaze's eyes, now.

"Yeah, I just thought that whole 'odd' thing was kind of offensive. My parents made it up—my name I mean. Or at least I think so," I blabbered, my face beginning to scrunch up because I could tell my words were coming out all funny.

"Are you scared of us?" Twig said with a slight smirk as if that was the goal he was trying to accomplish all along. It was rather difficult not to be intimidated when a giant butterfly was glaring at you from across the woods.

"Well, to be honest I think they are all a little scared of

us." Tio said, looking at her two brothers.

"Should we turn?" Twig asked the other two. He seemed annoyed, yet he was still staring into my eyes as if he were trying to read me somehow. I wondered what was so fascinating about them. If anything, you would think someone would go and stare at Cy's eyes.

They were such a mystery, the three of them. There was something odd about them and I definitely wanted to know more.

The Novus Proprius Chronicles

Chapter 6

After a bit of arguing about the butterfly version of evolving, which they called turning, they finally revealed their human forms to us. They stood around and argued about it for a bit, Twig arguing the most, though he was the one who'd mentioned it in the first place. Once they had all agreed on turning, however, I realized that they were all about the same age as us.

As they turned, their spiked wings slowly curved into their backs. All the fuzz slowly crept up, and gathered at the top of their heads, becoming their human hair. Their long tongues, now used to suck the life out of unwilling animals instead of nectar, became a small tongue. Their giant bug eyes slowly shrunk, creating a strange noise that sounded like someone was squeezing jelly out of a donut. Their heads shrunk, too, making them look deformed at first.

Once they had finally turned, they looked like they could have been werewolves, if they didn't have sharp teeth. On the corners of their mouths, they had a set of small fangs that pointed straight down. I noticed that even in human form they had a tendency to stare straight into your eyes. I wasn't sure what was more intimidating; a giant butterfly or a person with fangs. Another thing they had in common was cherry red eyes that somehow seemed to reflect the sunlight, almost like a mirror.

Tio was one of the most beautiful people I'd ever seen. She had a small and narrow face with high, well-defined cheek bones. Her hair was dark brown, almost black, and it fell in corkscrew curls down her back. It was like an endless waterfall of perfect curly hair that didn't seem to stop as it flowed down her hourglass figure.

Twig and Haze could have passed for twin supermodels, they looked so similar. They both had brown hair, like Tio, though Haze's had more of a reddish tint, whereas Twig's seemed a bit more golden. They both had well-defined cheekbones, much like Tio, though their jaw bones were wider, causing them to look more masculine.

Tio and her brothers were all very tall, almost supermodel tall, and they were all very skinny, also. They looked like they worked out often, though more on endurance. They had long lean muscles, rather than bulging arms and legs. All in all, they seemed like one of the most beautiful families I'd ever seen.

Cy, Blaze, and I all gawked at their beauty until Cy finally asked, "How old are you guys?"

"Like that's any of your business," Haze said, almost sounding hostile, as he gazed into my eyes.

"Gosh, attitude much?" I asked, looking down at the ground awkwardly. I wasn't quite sure how to handle an angry butterfly.

"It's not attitude," Haze said, in a rather feminine voice, making me assume he wasn't angry anymore. "It's called sass," he finished, snapping repeatedly and drawing a 'z' in the air, causing Tio and Twig to shake their heads in embarrassment.

Trying to completely ignore what I'd just seen, I asked, "Why do you guys have fangs?" I looked at the three of them, comparing their fangs, and noticed that Twig's were much larger than his brother's and sister's.

"Have you ever heard of vampires?" Twig asked, folding his arms across his chest. I noticed that as he spoke, his fangs seemed to look larger. *Creepy,* I thought to myself, and I couldn't help but notice Twig chuckle under his breath for some reason.

"Oh, I've read about them," Cy exclaimed, probably excited that there was something for her to talk about. "They are creatures of the night supposedly, and they can't go into the sunlight. They suck blood out of people and animals; they can turn into bats, and some other stuff. I don't know, I haven't memorized it all," she finished, still looking thrilled.

"Anyways," Twig mumbled, rolling his eyes. "We are like vampires—we drink blood, only we obviously don't turn into bats, and we can be in sunlight," he said, raising his arms up and looking at the sun. He glanced down at Cy, looking her straight in the eyes. My guess was he was trying to scare her, and it seemed to be working. Cy nervously shifted weight from foot to foot as he told us about their kind.

"Well, I guess we'll see you in the forests again sometime," Cy stuttered. "See ya!" she said anxiously, pulling at my sleeve to try and get me to leave with her.

"No, wait," I began, hoping they wouldn't leave. "How long have you guys been like this?" I asked, though I could have probably phrased it better. "I mean, how long has your kind existed?" I finished.

"As long as your kind has," Twig said, with a slight smirk, as if he realized this would be completely mindboggling news. I looked down at the ground, thinking, and wondering how on earth this could be possible.

"Why don't we hunt together?" Blaze suggested, trying to break the awkward silence.

"That would be fun," Tio said, sounding excited. She glanced at her brothers with an encouraging look, though it didn't seem like she needed to.

"What? No!" Cyprus yelled, shaking her head, almost as if the very idea gave her nightmares.

"Why not? Are you nervous?" Twig said, mockingly with a wicked grin. I could tell he was making her uncomfortable because he was still staring her straight into her eyes. As his gaze went from Cy's eyes, he rested it on me, then glanced down at my neck.

"Um, excuse you," I said, trying to cover up my neck.

"What?" he asked, looking baffled. *As if you don't know what I'm talking about,* I thought, accusingly.

"You're looking at my neck, you creep," I said, accusingly, still trying to use my clothes to cover myself up.

"Hey!" he exclaimed, looking at his brother and sister. "We completely forgot to tell them about our name situation," he said, most likely using this to his advantage to change the subject.

"Why don't you tell her—I mean them," Tio said, with a sly smirk as if sensing his helplessness.

Twig let out a hopeless sigh, as if he wished she could have told them but then began to explain. "Okay well, when we've turned and we're like this, we go by different names. That's why, when we're together, we have to agree to turn because if the 'others' find out we're here, let's just say it could end badly because we're not supposed to be on your island," he paused. "I go by Duke." He finished, though I wouldn't have expected him to go by that name.

"My real name is Byrd," the girl I had just earlier known as Tio said, raising her hand.

Haze looked at us reluctantly, almost as if his name was embarrassing. "My name is Gizmo," he said, looking awkwardly at the tree he was leaning on.

"Gizmo? What kind of name is that?" Cy asked, crossing her arms, causing her uneasiness to fade away and instead be replaced by playful mockery.

"What kind of name is Cyprus?" Haze, or now Gizmo asked, defensively.

"So, what names do you guys prefer?" I asked, trying to distract Cy and Gizmo from their banter.

"These ones," Byrd said, "they're our real names. The other ones are just nicknames," she finished. The name 'Byrd' really suited her for some reason.

"I'm leaving," Duke said, beginning to walk away.

"Where are you going?" Byrd asked anxiously, running after him.

"We need to start hunting, now. We're not even supposed to be here," Duke said, nervously, looking around.

"Why are you guys even here?" Blaze asked, looking at the three of them curiously.

"There's a food shortage on our island, so we thought we could come here for some," Gizmo explained. *There's not much food here either,* I thought to myself.

"I don't know about you, Cy, but I'm going with Duke," I began, and she gave me an accusing look as if I'd betrayed her. "If I get home late my parents will kill me. Plus we barely have any food," I explained to her, hoping she would understand. I ran after Duke, hoping he would take me with him.

"Hold on, Zaina," Blaze said, "I'm coming with you. My family needs food too. Plus I promised my pack I would bring them some," he said, pulling at Cyprus's sleeve to try and get her to come with. When she didn't move he looked at her confused and said, "Come on, Cy, I thought you loved hunting."

"I do when it's just us werewolves hunting!" she said, looking at Byrd, Gizmo, and Duke, worriedly.

"Don't worry, we only bite occasionally," Gizmo said with a smile as he helped Blaze pull her towards the rest of us.

"Fine," she said, giving in and catching up with the rest of us. She ran up and glared at Duke from behind me as if I was her shield from the big, bad world.

We began walking through the woods, in search of deer to hunt, however all we could find were small rodents and chipmunks. Until today, I had no idea there were other islands, and knowing that the other islands were having food shortages just like ours worried me.

We continued looking for food and I could see Cyprus slowly start to get used to the idea of being with the butterflies. Her shoulders began to loosen up and her hands relaxed from the fists they were nearly an hour ago. I couldn't figure out why they scared her so much.

Duke, most likely sensing her ease, decided to scare her half to death to make her uneasy again. He suddenly turned into his butterfly form and flew up into a tree faster than the speed of light. It was one of the most incredible things I'd ever seen, also one of the fastest. I heard Byrd gasp, most likely thinking about 'the others' who they seemed to be so worried about.

Once he was in the tree, he turned once more into human form and grabbed a small, albino chipmunk. Next thing we knew, he had jumped from the tree branch and was standing in front of Cy, sucking the blood out of the poor animal as it squealed and wriggled around to try and get free.

"You know, this could be you some day," he said, menacingly, with blood spilling out of the corner of his mouth.

At this point, he strongly resembled a rabid dog with they way his eyes were wide in cruel excitement. He was having way too much fun trying to scare the daylights out of poor Cyprus.

As Cy saw the poor albino, she shrieked and began to run away, looking green. Duke ran in front of her, not wanting to let her get away, and tossed the animal at her feet.

"That's disgusting!" she shrieked. "Stop it!" She pleaded.

"Leave her alone," I told Duke defensively, pushing him away. What was wrong with him? He didn't seem this cruel earlier. "Hey, hon, you okay?" I asked, kneeling down to Cyprus's level to see if she was okay. I tried to comfort her as I rubbed her back, but it didn't seem to be working.

"I think I'm going to puke," she said, still staring down at the animal. I couldn't quite figure it out. She was a werewolf and went hunting all the time. Why was this so difficult for her to accept? It was just an animal.

"Cyprus, we have to keep going," Byrd said, looking around nervously.

Suddenly, we all heard what sound like a stampede coming from afar. "Did you hear that?" Gizmo said in alarm, looking over his shoulder.

Then I recognized the sound. It was the sound of a pack of wolves coming for us. They had probably heard Cy scream, or were aware of the butterflies on the island. Either way, we all knew that we desperately needed to get away.

"They're gonna kill us!" Byrd said in alarm, looking at her brothers, hoping they would know what to do.

"What? Why?" Cy asked as she tore her attention from the chipmunk to look at Byrd; she seemed rather pale around the nose.

"There is a law against werewolves and butterflies talking much less going hunting together! They're worried about the species intermingling," she said, frantically, still looking around as if she couldn't figure out where the noise was coming from.

"Why didn't you think of that sooner?" Gizmo said, sounding almost annoyed. "Do they know who we are?" Gizmo asked, looking at Duke. The panic was beginning to make his voice louder than it should have been.

I looked over at Duke, wondering how he would know. Suddenly, he seemed to stiffen up, almost as if he were turning to stone. *What is happening,* I thought to myself. I walked up next to him and waved my hand in front of his face, wondering if he could still see me. I looked closer, and realized that his red eyes seemed to have turned a brick, red. Orange swirls were beginning to take over his eyes, and I couldn't figure out why.

"No, but they know we're here," he said, nodding at Byrd and Gizmo. Abruptly, they all turned into their butterfly forms.

For a second I thought they were all going to leave us in the dust, but then Gizmo said, "Quick! Get on my back," to Cy.

She hesitated for a moment then quickly ran over. Blaze immediately went over to Byrd, probably because he didn't seem to like Duke one bit. Of course that left me with the one person I really didn't want to be with—Duke.

It was odd, flying. Luckily we got away just in time. As soon as we were in the air, wolves with armor surrounded the small spot where we were standing just a few seconds ago.

The armor gleamed in the setting sun's beams. It was

almost as if the armor was begging for war. It was good we got to the cloud banks before they saw us. Some had bows and arrows strapped to their backs. While a few of them stayed in their wolf form, some of them evolved and started shooting anything that was moving in the sky. If it wasn't for Duke, Byrd, and Gizmo, we could all be dead.

"So, what is it like to fly for the first time?" Duke asked, curiously, looking over his shoulder and into my eyes.

"Kind of weird, but cool at the same time." I said, stuttering, looking down at the far-off ground. I didn't realize how high up we here. Then, I noticed Duke quickly looked down at my neck, and then at my cheek, for some reason, but not my eyes, almost as if he was ashamed. "Why do you keep doing that?" I asked, a little worried.

"Uh, doing what?" he asked, he looked forward again, which was a good thing because he manages to pass a giant tree we would have hit if he hadn't looked forward just in time.

"You keep looking at my neck. You seemed to try and avoid talking about it around the others earlier." I told him. I still found the idea of talking to a giant butterfly unnerving.

How could I not have known about their kind until now? I thought to myself. You would think they would teach something like that in school, along with the fact that there were other islands out there.

"Um, well. I guess—" he stuttered, not knowing how to respond.

"You're not used to being around werewolves, are you?" I asked, pushing for answers. I was getting tired of him avoiding my questions.

"No, not really. The last time I met a werewolf I, um," he began, hesitating. "I kinda killed him." He said, trying to look innocent but then looked away from me once again, as if he were ashamed.

"Oh," I said, nervously. "So, you're not planning on killing me are you?" I asked, hoping those weren't his plans.

"No, no, no! You're a nice werewolf. He was really annoying," he said with a smirk. *As if that's an excuse,* I thought laughingly, thinking of Bow for some reason. He then changed the subject as soon as he possibly could. "Wanna see something cool?" he asked, with a cruel grin, causing me not to trust him.

"What are you going to do?" I asked, alarmingly. I'd just met Duke and I didn't trust him, especially considering what he did to Cy earlier.

"It's a surprise, Rusty!" he said, laughingly.

"Rusty?" I asked in surprise. No one ever called me anything besides Zaina. I kind of liked the idea of a nickname.

"Yeah, Rusty—because you have so many freckles," he said with a smile. "Now, do you wanna see something?" he asked as we both laughed at the same time.

"Uh, sure, I guess," I said, waiting for what I thought could have been my death. I was almost scared to see what he was going to do.

As we flew, Duke suddenly decided to turn, leaving us free-falling. I wanted to scream but something told me not to. It felt as if my stomach were being left high up in the orange lit sky. Looking up at the setting sun was actually quite beautiful. It reminded me of how I always felt around the fire. There was just something about fires that was both mysterious and beautiful at the same time. The fire just always had a different story to tell.

We fell for a while, but I became nervous as I noticed

the ground getting closer and closer. "Oh, okay, I think I'm good now!" I frantically yelled, hoping he could hear me through all the wind as he flew in the other direction as me. I was about to hit the ground when I saw him land. He quickly brought something over to where I was falling and as I hit the ground, I landed on something almost fluffy. The fall was hard, but not as bumpy as I had expected it to be.

"Oh my gosh! You gave me a heart attack!" I yelled at him as I tried to get up. However, my head was spinning and I found the task quite challenging. My knees buckled out in front of me as my body tried to get used to walking again.

"You said you wanted to see something, so I let you feel what it was like to land…the hard way," he said, apologetically, though all he did was smirk.

It took me a while to get used to walking again. There was this after effect of flying that kind of made you dizzy. Feeling so dizzy made me forget to ask what it was I landed on. All I knew was that it was soft. It was also kind of hard, but comfortable to land on, I guess. I never found out what it was that I'd landed on, or how it managed to go unnoticed for so many years on such a tiny island.

I looked around and realized he had dropped me a few feet away from my house. I wasn't quite sure how he knew where I lived, however, which kind of made me worried. "Here, take this so your folks won't be that mad," Duke said, handing me a sack. I looked inside it and saw that there were three rabbits inside.

"How did you know?" I asked, curiously. I didn't remember telling him my family needed food.

"I heard you talking to Cy," he said simply, shrugging and putting his hands in his pockets.

"I can't take this, what are you going to eat?" I said handing him the sack, even though he refused to take it.

"Oh, it's okay. I don't live with my parents anymore so I'm going to go hunting again," he said, smiling. Though he seemed excited to hunt more, you could tell he was extremely bored.

"You're lucky; you get to do whatever you want," I said turning to my cave. Before I went inside, I looked back and said "See you again sometime in the woods," while waving him goodbye.

"…bye," he muttered, emotionlessly. He almost seemed

disappointed that I had to go. I would have been happy for the new friends I'd made today if it weren't for the laws against us hanging out. However, I had to admit—flying was pretty fun.

I was almost scared to walk into my own cave because I thought my parents would be mad at me, but it was starting to get dark. If I didn't get into the cave soon, my parents would be even madder at me then I'm sure they already were. "Hey guys!" I said happily, walking into my cave. I went to sit by the fire. "Or should I say guy?" I laughed. I put the sack next to my dad. "Where's mom?" I asked, but my father seemed to cringe at the sound of her name. The look on my dad's face was horrifying. Something was wrong.

Chapter 7

"I'm so sorry," my father began. "But your mother and I were attacked by the butterflies. They took her with them," he said, sobbing. I immediately began to sob as well as fear and worry began to make the back of my throat burn and my head feel like it was dropping while my body was standing still.

"What happened to her? Is she okay?" I asked, worriedly, as a strange pain in my chest began to form—almost as if my crying was causing the muscles in my chest to tighten up.

"I am so sorry to tell you this, but," he hesitated looking down at his hands. "Your mother is dead," he said simply, though his voice was cracking as he sat there, crying uncontrollably.

From the corner of my eye, I could see Duke looking into the cave after hearing all the commotion from outside. I got up and started angrily walking towards the door.

"Where are you going? Zaina? Zaina! Stay here!" I heard my father yelling though I didn't listen. I didn't want to; I was furious. Mad at the butterflies, mad at my father, mad at myself—and for some reason at Duke. I knew it wasn't his fault, but I needed someone to blame it on. I'd never handled grief well and it seemed like anger was usually the way I handled it.

"You!" I yelled, accusingly. "You and your kind! Why? Why did you have to kill her?" I said, sobbing, and continuously trying to hit him, though he just continued to block me.

"Zaina, it'll be okay," he said, reassuringly. "I'm not the one you're mad at, remember? I didn't do this," he said calmly, almost as if he was used to grief.

Then, sorrow washed over me once more. I wasn't normally the type to seek comfort, but this was a situation I had never experienced before. I had experienced grief, but never like this. I started feeling dizzy because of all the commotion. I knew that my dad was hiding something; I just knew it. I could feel it in my bones. And there was also a feeling of guilt. I felt that maybe if I would have been there to help tonight, I could have saved her. But instead, I was out hanging out with friends and the very species that killed my mother.

The pain in my lungs continued to worsen and my head

began getting dizzier and dizzier with time. I began to fall forward, and eventually Duke caught me and I was about to fall to the ground. The pain in my lungs and anger for the butterflies was the last thing I could remember.

Duke

I never expected Rusty to fall into my arms like that. And I really didn't expect her to pass out. *How am I going to explain this to her dad?* I thought, frantically. Rusty had been yelling pretty loud, so chances where that he'd heard her and would be out any moment.

I looked down at her; I knew I couldn't just leave her in the cold dirt. Then I noticed something—it looked like someone had been dragged off. There was also a puddle of blood. Near the puddle, it almost looked like it had rained only in a specific area. Then my over-imaginative brain wondered; what if those were someone's tears?

I bent over to pick her up. Once she we in my arms, I couldn't help but notice that she was just lying there as if she were a rag doll. It was incredible hard to resist the urge to bite her neck as her head was bent back, making it seem like on open invitation. However, Rusty was my friend. *Killing her will not make you two closer*, my inner me said.

I carried her into her cave and noticed that it was darker and drearier then I remembered it. Her father, who looked a lot older then I would have expected, sat by the fire with his head in his hands. *I miss this place*, I thought to myself.

"Umm, sir?" I asked, cautiously, trying to hide my fangs.

Her dad looked up in confusion, probably expecting someone more feminine. Of course, the first this he noticed was the fangs. *Great job*, I lectured myself, *did you really think this would be easy?*

"What are you doing here?" he asked accusingly. I couldn't tell if he remembered me or not.

"Um, well—Zaina," I said, trying to hand her to her father, though he just stood there, staring me down. "She passed out," I tried to explain, though it didn't seem to be working. If there was anything I'd learned from the past, it was that nothing could get through this man's head that he didn't want put there himself.

He walked up closer to me, still staring me in the eyes, glaring at me. As he looked down at his daughter, inquisitively, I couldn't quite figure out what he was doing. It wasn't until he examined both sides of her neck that I realized he was making sure I hadn't gotten myself a snack.

"Put her here," he said, emotionlessly, pointing to a straw mat that was lying near the fire. *That's a little close*, I told myself, warily. I pushed it over with the side of my foot and I heard her father grunt quietly as he simply watched. *No, I don't need help,* I thought, looking at her father, *thanks for asking.*

"So, how do you know my daughter?" he asked curiously. "I mean, you obviously don't know her from school," he said, sarcastically, though I couldn't figure out why.

I was amazed that he was so calm around me after what had just happened to his wife. Although he was smiling, I could still see how the tears had stained his eyes and cheeks. Red rings surrounded his eyes and I could tell his was hard for him. Love was a painful thing—I personally thought it was only meant to destroy so I usually avoided it completely.

"Okay, I know it may be against the law but we were hunting today. She was with her two friends and we thought we could help them hunt," I said, feeling like I needed to explain things. "Not that Zaina needs help or anything," I said, nervously babbling.

"Hum," was all he said, as he took a small buck knife from behind his back and set it down next to him. "Interesting," he added, smiling as if knowing he had managed to scare the daylights out of me. *He was ready to stab me,* I told myself, *he was really gonna do it!* I couldn't help but feel threatened now.

"We did get surrounded, though. A pack of wolves heard her friend, Cyprus, scream but we managed to fly away," I said, imitating how we flew with my hand flattened.

"Did th—" he started, eyes widening in fear. I knew exactly what he was going to ask. It was the same question anyone would have asked.

"See us? No, they didn't see any of our faces," I said, reassuring him. I was trying to speak as proper as I could, for some reason. I wasn't even sure myself, yet I think her dad could tell how hard I was trying.

"Really, you don't have to try and impress me. I'm already impressed just by the fact that you didn't just leave her out there," he said, causing me to wonder if he did, in fact, remember me.

"Oh," I said blankly, wondering why I'd wasted so much time trying to act proper.

"You mind if I ask you something?" he asked, looking at me curiously.

"Sure?" I said, cautiously, though I wasn't sure if the answer would be something he would want to hear.

"You're her 'shadow' aren't you?" he asked, sounding more enthusiastic then I think he should have sounded. He sat forward in his chair as if he were an eager five year old ready for story time.

"I," I said, though I hesitated. We weren't supposed to tell anyone. How he knew about the prophesies was beyond me, though it did cause me to worry some. *Who else has he told?* I asked myself.

"Oh come on," he said, punching me in the shoulder slightly. "You really think I don't know about the prophesies? I'm her father for crying out loud," he said, giving me a questioning look as if I should have known better. "You are, aren't you?" he almost seemed to yell slightly, sounding all too eager.

"Yeah, sure," I said, shrugging, finally giving in to his pushiness. "So when do you think she'll be better?" I asked, as he tucked some of Zaina's hair behind her ear.

"She'll probably wake up tomorrow. You're welcome to stay here if you're worried," he said, smiling at me. I guess he liked me much better knowing I was her 'shadow.'

"Um, would that be a problem?" I asked, looking around the cave for something more comfortable to sit on. I couldn't let someone as important as Rusty be unattended in her situation. She had a great destiny ahead of her and the world depended on it.

"Sure," he said, sounding a little too friendly. "But, you have to stay up all night," he said. Though he sounded sarcastic, I eventually found out he really wasn't kidding.

"Okay?" I said, sounding a little confused. "You can sleep if you like. I'll wake you up when she does," I said, this time causing him to laugh.

"I guess this is one of those times when I'm just going to have to trust one of my daughter's shadows," he said, sounding amazed. "Gosh, I never thought my daughter would ever have a shadow!" he exclaimed, staring at the ceiling as if he were deep in thought.

There was something odd about the way he was acting. Wasn't a husband who just lost his wife supposed to be sad and grieving rather than happy and chipper?

"Don't worry, I only bite occasionally." I teased, using Gizmo's oh-so-famous line. His expression was unreadable now making me wonder if he thought I was being serious.

"Ha, good night," he said, sarcastically, lying down on a straw mattress next to the fire. I was expecting him to turn around to check on Zaina, but in the end he didn't.

Zaina

It was in the middle of the night, possibly early morning after I had woken up. My head felt painfully heavy and everything else seemed to hurt, as well. When my eyes were no longer blurry with sleep, I looked over and saw Duke sitting next to me. Dad was sleeping on one of the mattresses right across from me though I was surprised he would let Duke in the cave after the events of this evening.

"Duke?" I mumbled, rubbing the remaining sleepy blurriness out of my eyes.

"Rusty, you're awake! Oh thank God!" He exclaimed happily. I saw him reach over me to wake up Dad. At first, Dad pushed Duke's hand away, not wanting to wake up, but then he suddenly shot up.

"She's awake?" he yelled, eyes wide in excitement.

"Hey," I mumbled. "Why are you yelling?" I said, managing to giggle a tad. I stopped as soon as I started, however. There was still that pain in my lungs, only it had worsened as I passed out.

"Sorry, I'm just so happy you're awake," he said, smiling. He glanced over at Duke, also smiling as if he was proud of him; I felt like there was something I was missing, but I was too out of it to ask.

I tried to sit up, but found that the pain in my chest made it nearly impossible. Then I could feel Duke grab my left arm and my dad grab my right. Together as a team, they pulled me up. *Whoa, that's amazing,* I thought.

"Thanks," I mumbled, smiling at them both as they sat next to the fire.

Again, Duke was looking into my eyes with those bright

red, sparking eyes. I almost felt like someone was trying to break through a type of shield in my head—like they were trying to invade my privacy or by any chance read my mind. If it was Duke, I don't know. I just know that all this was making my head go berserk.

"You're welcome," they both said almost in unison. Once Dad noticed Duke looking into my eyes, he shot him a protective glare causing Duke to hurriedly look away.

I sat there laughing at the two of them and their awkward interactions when suddenly, it hit me. *The dream,* I thought to myself in alarm. It wasn't really a dream—more like a series of events that really seemed to be happening. There was also the faint sense of being watched throughout the whole dream as if I was getting this dream from someone else. As if I was meant to get this dream. Almost as if it would benefit me in some way.

"I had the weirdest dream while I blacked out!" Duke leaned forward to listen. "I dreamt about a girl named Ember. She was supposedly a witch," I informed them, not quite knowing why. I noticed my dad was trying to fake a confused look, probably because witches were said to be evil and we weren't supposed to spend too much time looking into them.

"A witch is someone who can do things like make deer appear out of nowhere, or move things with his or her mind." Duke explained as if he was actually buying my dad's look.

"Mmhmm," my dad said with his hand on his chin. I was surprised how calm he was being around Duke. I couldn't help but wonder if he had his old buck knife in his pocket, just in case. *He probably does,* I thought to myself, amusingly.

"She and some girl were eating something, but I couldn't tell what it was. The one girl was talking about these dreams that she had. She asked the other girl, Ember, if she would help her get rid of them. And then Ember told her no. Isn't that weird?" For a second, I thought my dad was seeing a ghost. "Dad?" I asked, wondering if it was something I said. Duke and I both turned around to see what my father was staring blankly at.

I wasn't quite sure what I was expecting to see, but what I did see was not what I had imagined. Behind us was another giant butterfly along with something white as pearls that soon disappeared before I could get a good look at it.

My eyes shot around our cave, looking for a weapon. There were so many things I didn't know about these creatures—especially how to kill them. There always had to be some trick way to do it, and I didn't know what to do in this situation.

I looked over at Duke, worriedly, hoping he would know how to kill this thing. "We don't have to kill it," he whispered, almost as if he's read my mind. *Well then how do you get it to go away,* I thought, almost annoyed.

Suddenly, Duke turned into his butterfly form and charged at the beast. Its eyes widened as if flew away, whimpering. As Duke turned back into his human form and looked at the two of us, he said, "All you gotta do is show that this is your territory." *That would have been nice to know when they were attacking my mom,* I thought to myself, still blaming myself for her death. I could have helped, had I been here.

My dad walked over to Duke, who wasn't expecting it, to give him a big hug. "Oh thank you! You saved us both," he said, a little over dramatic. I think Dad was starting to like Duke, though the look on Duke's face as my father squeezed him half to death made me think the feeling wasn't mutual.

Chapter 8

Despite the events of the night before, my dad was convinced that still I needed to go to school. So, I got ready like any other day, though today seemed so much emptier then all the other days.

I was so used to my mom waking me up. I was used to my mom making breakfast over the fire, but now that she wasn't there anymore, it felt like a big, empty hole in the middle of my chest. Almost like someone had carved out a piece of my heart. Never would my mom ever be able to hold me again. I would never be able to hear her soft, sweet voice to comfort me when I was having problems in school, or with friends. I didn't have her there to even scold me when I did something wrong. I wasn't sure how I was going to live the rest of my life without someone as influential as her in my life. She was my role model, and best friend, and now both of those things were gone.

"Bye Dad," I said, sadly. "See you after school," I said, as I waved him goodbye.

As I began walking through the woods to school I heard a far off voice yell, "Wait! Wait!" I looked back and noticed

Duke running to try and get me.

"Oh, hey Duke. I actually forgot you were here," I said, chuckling under my breath. Though I had just met him last night, there was something about him that was so familiar and comfortable that it felt like I'd known him for years.

"Yeah, I kinda noticed," he said with the slightest attitude. "I was just getting some breakfast when I saw you walking. Mind if I join you?" he asked, pointing to the path in front of me that led to the school.

"Uh, sure," I said with a smile. I began to move my side bangs from the left to right, trying to decide which way to put them.

"I think you should put them to the left," he said, laughing at me but then looking away and down at the ground.

"W-what?" I asked, slightly stuttering in surprise. No one could ever figure out the reason behind me moving my bangs; they all just thought I was weird.

He repeated himself again, slightly chuckling, as we began walking towards the school together.

"No, I mean—how did you know what I was doing?" I asked, still in amazement, though I wasn't quite sure why. I could tell by Duke's laugh that my face was printed with confusion and that he, for some reason, found it extremely amusing.

"There was just something about the face you made that made it rather obvious that you were uncertain about something. And you know, since you were moving your bangs back and forth, I figured," he trailed off, not finishing what he was saying. Then I noticed his eyes were no longer on me, they were looking at something behind me, seeming almost mesmerized.

I turned around as quickly as I could, worried it might be another wolf that had it out for me. However, once I looked behind me, I noticed it was the same blurry, pearly white figure I'd seen last night. Just as yesterday, I tried to see what it was. However, as soon as it looked like it was coming closer, it seemed to vanish into thin air. Today, I managed to see something I hadn't noticed last night; a horn.

In the end I was, as usual, the one with the baffled look on my face. *Figures,* I thought to myself. Duke was always so perfect and I often envied him for that.

I kept looking over where the blob had been until I noticed that Duke was waving his hand in front of my face. "You look like you've seen a ghost or something," he said, acting as if he hadn't seen it.

"Or something," I mumbled, practically unable to think. "So," I said moving my gaze from where the white blob had stood to were Duke was aimlessly walking next to me. "Why do you think I should have them to the left?" I asked as aimlessly as he was walking. I was trying to think about anything but that strange figure I'd just seen.

"I don't know, I just like them better that way," he said, shrugging, looking down at the ground.

"It's just a question," I said, laughingly. It was kind of cute how defensive he could get sometimes.

"Your mom was pretty important to you, wasn't she?" he asked, most likely trying to change the subject. I looked down at my attire and remembered. For a split second, I had somehow almost forgotten she was gone. Guilt surged over me, though I answered his question.

"She was my mom, after all. I don't know about your kind, but my kind wears all black to honor our dead," I said, looking down at the ground, still feeling kind of guilty. Then I remembered something I had read in a book a long time ago. One major thing humans and werewolves had in common were the rituals of burial.

"But how do you know that," he hesitated, "that she's dead I mean," he said, as if hinting towards something I didn't know yet. I looked at him, bewildered. "I mean, for all you know she could still be alive, and you just don't know it," he shrugged, putting his hands in his pockets. He could tell the conversation was turning into an argument so he shut up for once. "Look, I'm sorry," he said, trying to apologize, though I was a little too angry to listen. "I didn't mean it like that; I just meant to say that you never know."

"Do you know something I don't know?" I asked, suspiciously. This conversation wasn't one you normally had after a family member had died.

"Nope," he said, eye widening, as if he were in trouble. Seeing that the conversation was getting nowhere, we decided that it would be best just to walk the rest of the way in silence.

The silence wasn't broken until we reached my school.

"Well, there it is. The little school of Meadows where literally everyone goes," I said, pointing to the medium sized, kind of rough looking school in front of me. As Duke stood there examining the school, I noticed Cyprus walking by.

Her eyes widened as she saw Duke, and ran into the school at a surprising pace. "Great," I began, looking at Duke disapprovingly. "Your little chipmunk thing yesterday scared the bedoozies out of her," I said, still looking at him.

"Bedoozies?" he asked, chuckling softly.

"Yes, bedoozies. It's my word," I said laughingly, which caused him to laugh again. "Oh great," I began, seeing Ruby and a bunch of her friends looking over and giggling at Duke like most girls did when they though a guy was attractive.

"What?" he said, though I could tell he saw them, too, considering he was looking at all of them from head to toe.

"Oh, nothing! It's just Ruby, the one with the red hair over there. She's a nutcase and I can't stand her," I said, frowning and crossing my arms over my chest.

"Don't worry, she's not my type." He said, smirking at me before he began to walk away.

"Why should I care?" I mumbled to myself before yelling it to Duke considering I really did want to know why it mattered.

"Good bye, Rusty," he said, waving and winking at me for reasons I couldn't figure out. Later, I found out it was to make Ruby and her friends jealous, though I was still confused at the time. Then, as quick at the blob had gone Duke vanished also.

As I was walking into my classroom, I could feel Ruby's pinprick stare from across the room. I could tell that Duke's little winking thing really did work. I then began to wonder if she'd seen the fangs. I really hoped she hadn't because it could give me the opportunity to scare the mess out of her. There was just something so satisfying about messing with Ruby; almost like giving a doctor the taste of his own medicine.

"What's up with all the black, goth girl?" Ruby said, looking at my outfit, resting her eyes at my neck. I looked down and suddenly noticed a small, blackish-purple diamond shaped pendant on a gold chain hanging around my neck. Up until this point I had no idea I was wearing it, much less how I'd gotten it.

"My mom died yesterday," I mumbled, just loud enough for her to hear me. For the first time ever, I noticed Ruby look down in sorrow, as if she felt bad for me.

"Oh my gosh. Sorry, I—I didn't know," she said, hesitating. I could tell she really felt bad for me, though I wasn't sure why. In the history I'd known her, I never once heard her say sorry. "My condolences," she finished, lowering her head.

"Holy crap!" I suddenly heard Cy yell as she ran into the classroom. "Why are you, of all people, hanging out with someone like him?" she questioned me, almost angrily.

"No need to over react," I said, calmingly. "Who are you talking about?" I finished, innocently.

"Oh you know very well who I am talking about, missy. I'm talking about Duke!" she almost yelled. Suddenly Ruby's head shot up and she was back to herself.

"Oh! Was that who you were walking to school with? He was hot!" she said, turning in her seat towards us as if she wanted to have an actual conversation with us. I shut my eyes. *I do not need this right now,* I thought to myself.

"Yes," I said, through clenched teeth, looking over my

shoulder at Ruby. I wasn't quite sure why I was so angry.

"Is he single?" she asked desperately, her eyes widening. You would think a girl like her wouldn't have trouble getting a guy.

"Yeah, but he said you weren't his type, sorry," I told her as I walked over to her seat. I didn't know why I was defensive all of a sudden.

"Fine, whatever," she said, looking at Gigi as she walked into class, and then glanced back at me. "You and me need to talk at lunch, though," she finished, as if we were enemies in preschool who were stealing each other's belongings.

"Okay," I said, shrugging my shoulders. *Finally*, I thought. Soon, I would be able to give her a taste of her own medicine. Too bad it was going to be a failed attempt to scare her off.

The Novus Proprius Chronicles

Chapter 9

I sat there, waiting for school to end, partially listening to Ms. Gigi lecture us on the structure of humans, and partially thinking about that fire from yesterday. I couldn't help but wish I'd stayed when it beckoned me to sit by it.

Then there was a long string of questions that swirled through my mind like cotton candy being made fresh at a street fair. Would I have been able to stop the butterflies that attacked Mom and Dad? How is it that Dad didn't get hurt and Mom got killed? Why would they have taken her? Would things have gone different if I were there? Why did they attack in the first place?

I was staring out the window, deep in thought, when Ms. Gigi asked me a question without me knowing it. Suddenly, I noticed that I was being mesmerized by that strange white figure once again as it hide behind a tree, almost as if it were watching me.

Out of the corner of my eye, I noticed Ms. Gigi looking where I was and, for a second, I thought she saw it too. I couldn't hear much, but suddenly I heard a small voice in the back of my mind say "Pay attention, this is important."

The voice was difficult to understand at first, almost as if it were a mix of genders. I couldn't tell if it was male or female. Perhaps that's why I felt so confused.

"Pay attention to what?" I mumbled to myself, though it must not have been as quiet as I had intended it to be once I realized everyone was suddenly looking at me, confused.

"I'm sorry what?" Gigi asked, scrunching her forehead together, showing her worry wrinkles that I'd never noticed before.

I tore my attention away from the figure and looked up at Gigi, dazed. I was surprised to see her kneeling right in front of my desk, though it seemed just a second ago she was standing at the front of the room, talking to all of us.

"What do you want?" I asked, with a slight growl. For reasons I couldn't fathom, I suddenly became extremely aggressive and angry. For a split second I almost wanted to kill Ms. Gigi, and I couldn't figure out why. It wasn't until I realized what I was thinking that I managed to cool off a little bit.

"Honey?" she said, looking at me worriedly. "What's wrong?" she asked, as if she knew that it wasn't my fault I was suddenly so angry. I could hear sympathy pouring from her voice, almost as if she understood what was happening better then I did.

"Sorry," I managed to stutter as I reverted back to myself. "My mom died yesterday," I said with a pause, looking down at my desk. "I guess I'm just having a tough time coping." I heard a few people in the room gasp every so slightly. It wasn't normal for people to die on our island and not have everyone know about it right away.

"You never told me that," Cy said, to my surprise beginning to tear up.

I noticed Blaze look over at Cy and roll his eyes as if sorrow was something he was used to; almost as if he expected it from life. I looked into his eyes and I could see pain. It was like he understood what I was going through. It made me wonder if he'd lost a family member as well. There weren't many people on our island who had a constant sense of dread to their personality. Almost as if he expected sadness and misery in his life.

Richard, Zaina's father

I still couldn't believe what I had done. I hadn't killed Ivy, but what I did could have been considered murder. I had no idea what Zaina would have done if she found out the truth about what happened to her mother. Though I loved Ivy, I did what was necessary to keep everyone else safe, and to set Zee on the right path.

I saw Duke walking down a small path in the woods; the woods were Ivy and I had met as teenagers. All the memories were flowing back as if they were somehow liquid pain.

I remember the first time she and I actually met. It was a normal day as always, but the birds had been chirping a little louder than usual that day. It began to rain in the middle of all of it, once we got lost in the woods. There was something about her bright, luminous eyes that day that just made me feel safe around her. But now she was gone, and Zee would change so much because of my hopeless lies.

I ran up to Duke, and noticed something. He was just about as tall as me. "You're tall," I said, smiling, attempting small talk.

"What do you want?" he asked, seeming a little angry as

he continued walking with his hands in his pockets.

"Well," I began, "I was wondering if you could—if you could watch out for Zaina for a while," I finished, slightly stuttering. Duke gave me an odd look. I knew what he was thinking. Something along the lines of, *Why would you even leave in the first place?* "I'm leaving for a while. I'll be back soon. Well, in a couple of months or so," I shrugged, hoping he wouldn't ask any questions.

"Why?" he asked, looking confused; I couldn't blame the boy.

"Well, Zaina is supposed to do something which she can't do if I'm standing in her way," I tried to explain though he seemed confused.

"Well, I don't mind watching out for Zaina seeing as she's all important or whatever, but I need to know why you're leaving. You know she'll ask," he said, knowing my daughter all too well.

"Well, let's just say she's going to find out soon. Now, do you mind looking after her and making sure she goes to school and starts training?" I asked, hoping that my intuition about this boy was correct and that I could trust him. I'd only known this young man for about a day, after all. But knowing his role in the prophecies I felt like he would take good care of my little girl.

"Sure, when are you leaving?" he asked, as if he already knew the answer—soon. However, I didn't answer. I could tell he wasn't happy, but in the end it really didn't matter. This wasn't about him, it was about Zaina.

"I'm going to write you a note that you *have* to keep. It's just in case Zaina gets into trouble, which knowing her she probably will," I paused again. "It's so the teachers don't kill you when they see you," I said, calmly. He was taking this all surprisingly well. Then I noticed he wasn't paying attention to me, he was staring off in some direction as if he saw something. "You alright?" I asked, waving my hand in front of his face.

"It's," he began, trying to get his attention back to me and away from whatever he was looking at. "It's nothing," he finished, clearing his throat as if he'd just witnessed something that was hard to swallow. "So, what should I tell Zaina when she gets home?" he finished, as if trying to get his mind off of the incident that had just happened.

"Just tell her that," I began, rubbing my head, thinking of the best thing to say. "I guess just tell her I had to leave for her own good," I finished, shrugging. "Oh, and don't forget to tell her that I love her too," I added, hoping she wouldn't hate me too much for leaving her at a time like this.

"Okay," Duke said, solemnly. We began walking back to my cave in silence. I tried to start a conversation every once in a while, though the boy seemed too deep in thought to really concentrate on a specific topic.

Once we got back, I began cooking a squirrel over the fire that I'd just caught earlier that morning. Meanwhile, Duke sat on the ground, reading the letter looking puzzled and challenged; as if he couldn't figure out why this would do Zaina any good. I wasn't even sure why I was supposed to leave. All I knew was that they had told me it was a good time to leave, and I was afraid of what would happen if I didn't take their advice.

I sat there thinking about the letter, wondering if it was good enough. *Maybe I should re-write it,* I thought to myself, gravely. I remembered writing it as soon as Zaina had left for school. I wrote:

Dear Ms. Gigi,

I am writing this note to let you know that Duke will be taking care of Zaina for the time being. If there is any trouble, just call Duke in and tell him what he needs to do. Please do not kill him; he is only here to help Zaina. I know it may be against the law to interact with the other species, but please excuse the fact that he is a butterfly just this once. They told me to leave, and I must obey them. However, I cannot leave my daughter alone without someone to look out for her. You of all people should know that.

Richard

P.S. Don't mind Zaina's sudden behavior changes. They will develop into amazing talents that may help her save the world. And don't forget; you play a major role in this too. Be sure to do your part.

Thanks.

I observed Duke from across the room and could tell he knew something fishy was going on. Almost as if he knew Zee was going to get in trouble. As if he knew he would have to give Ms. Gigi the letter. Judging by his face, there were a lot of things that they hadn't told him yet; many things he would eventually find out.

"So, like I said, if you don't have this note with you when they call you in, they will kill you," I said, as simply as if we were talking about learning to ride a bike. He looked up from the letter, looking dazed, which made me wonder if he'd even heard me.

His facial expression changed to understanding, and he simply said, "I know." He seemed all right with it, somehow. "What do you mean, 'you play a major role in this too'?" he asked, even though he should already know the answer to that question.

"Look, there is a long story behind the reason why I'm leaving and I don't really have time to explain it. Not only that, but I'm not really supposed to talk about it to anyone. So please, just watch out for her," I said, looking to change the subject, but Duke's face let me know I wasn't getting off that easy.

"I got time," he said, simply, shrugging his shoulders. "And I'm pretty good at keeping secrets," he finished, pulling out a knife from his pocket and beginning to play with it in his hands.

"Don't you have something better to do?" I asked, feeling rather annoyed. Again, I was trying to change the subject, but the words just wouldn't come.

"No, not really. Although flying may sound like something that's really fun and something you could do for a long time, it's not. Especially not when you've been flying your whole life," he said, rolling his eyes.

"Okay then, you asked. And now you'll get it. You want to know everything? I'll tell you," I said, pausing like I always did when I wasn't certain about how someone was going to react to something. "Oh and might I add—most of it's not gonna be pretty. I've had to do *a lot* of things I'm not proud of," When I had finished, Duke just nodded, acceptingly.

Zaina

It took a long time for me to settle my mind on school, especially considering all the things Gigi seemed to be talking about were so incredibly dull. It wasn't until she started talking about how the world was before that I really began to pay attention. After a short lecture on the life of a human, Ms. Gigi said, "Okay, guys, now we'll start talking about how the human race came to an end," she finished, seeming chipper and delightful as usual.

That's odd, I thought. Yesterday, she had trouble talking about those things being gone. Today, however, she seemed more like us, not really caring about those things that existed so long ago.

"So," Gigi began before she was interrupted by the opening door. At first she glared at the door as if thinking, *how could you interrupt me,* but then she realized who it was.

Mrs. Heads, the principle, walked through the door followed by a boy. Her deep brown, almost black eyes stared us all down as she walked through the door. Her furrowed brows were surrounded by wrinkles, making her look much older than she was. Her grey hair was pulled up in a high bun, making it almost impossible to see the boy walking behind her. However, once she stood with both feet in the room, I could finally see his face.

Much like Cy, he had some of the palest blonde hair I'd ever seen. Looking at it closer, however, I realized it wasn't blonde, it was literally white. His face seemed incredibly familiar to me, almost like I'd met him before though I was sure I hadn't. He had a thin face, much like the rest of him. He had small cheekbones, making him look ever so slightly Asian, possibly even a little feminine, though I wasn't going to tell him that. He had beautiful baby blue eyes, the type that made girls jealous.

"So sorry Ms. Gigi," Mrs. Heads said, grinning wickedly at Gigi who simply rolled her eyes. "As crazy as this may sound, we have a new student," she said, monotonously though she seemed a little less grim then usual.

As the new boy looked curiously around the room, I couldn't help but notice his eyes rest on Cy. I looked over at her and noticed her face turn cherry red as he continued to look at her, up and down, for many moments.

I suddenly heard a low, protective growl come from behind me, a seat or two over. I looked back to see Blaze, looking utterly jealous, as he sat there glaring at the new boy. Judging by Cy's face and this new kid, I could tell they both really seemed to like each other's looks, and Blaze did not seem at all happy with that idea.

"Just great," I heard Bow mumble under his breath, though I wasn't sure what he was worried about.

"Hi," the new kid said, waving at the five of us as we sat in our old chairs. His voice seemed unusually deep for someone with a face like his.

Ms. Gigi and Mrs. Head talked quietly to themselves at the doorway for a few moments while the new guy just stood there looking at us with a kind of eerie grin. It was almost like he was judging us and our ability to hunt or communicate or something, I wasn't sure. But something about him seemed judgmental and I didn't like it.

As Mrs. Heads left and Ms. Gigi walked to her desk, the new boy began walking around the room picking up people's stuff, and looking at them with that same judgmental look. I could tell Ms. Gigi disliked this interruption. However, judging by the constant glances he kept giving her, he was just doing it to test her patience along with ours.

"Why don't you take a seat," Gigi said, though it wasn't a suggestion. It was obvious she was annoyed by him, just as I was. Especially considering he simply stood there, examining my ink, continuously looking disapproving. "You'll sit here," she said, pointing to the desk behind me. *Just great*, I thought to myself.

"Cool," he said, sarcastically, shrugging his shoulders and walking to his desk sluggishly. As he sat down, he began to look around the room as if thinking, '*wow, what a dump.*' He began to whistle some kind of a tune as he looked around the room; one I knew I'd heard before but couldn't quite pinpoint.

As if knowing the new boy was going to find introductions a joke, Gigi hesitantly said, "Um, we usually introduce ourselves to the class." She folded her arms across her chest, probably expecting a snide remark in return. For a split second, it almost seemed like they knew each other.

"What are we? Second graders?" he said, with a foul grin as if making others feel of lesser value was enjoyable.

"Well," she said, rolling her eyes. My guess was that she

was trying to ignore him as best she could. "We may have to do this after lunch if you don't start soon," she finished, hoping that people knowing his name was incentive enough to start talking.

"I'll wait till after," he said matter-of-factly, slouching back and putting his feet on the back on my chair.

"Why?" she asked through pearly white, clenched teeth. I almost felt bad for her; I didn't think I could handle rowdy wolves that were simply disobedient and disrespectful.

"'Don't really feel like talking about it," he said, examining and biting at his nails. Ms. Gigi looked around the room as if to find something else to talk about.

"Fine then," she said, giving in to his stubbornness, to my surprise.

With the time left, the five of us who weren't new told everyone our names all over again as if it were the first day of school. I couldn't help but find it amusing as the new kid began laughing hysterically as Bow told us his name once again, and then kindly explaining that if we didn't call him by his nickname he would hunt us down and possibly murder us. *That only makes me want to call him Bocepheus even more,* I thought to myself.

I couldn't help but think it was cute that when it was Cy's turn she began to stutter as she looked at the new boy. Following her two rosy red cheeks were two overprotective eyes from Blaze which was also slightly adorable.

By the time lunch came around, the new kid with spiky hair still wouldn't tell us his name. Whenever someone would ask he would simply say that we would have to wait till after lunch. He said he liked to build suspense.

As Gigi walked with us down to the cafeteria, I couldn't help but think about the satisfaction I would feel after I thoroughly scared the living hell out of Ruby. What made it even better was the fact that Ms. Gigi decided to put us in assigned seats because of the new kid. I couldn't help but wonder if she was simply hoping we would finally get a name out of him if he was surrounded by inquisitive and slightly pushy students. However, to my dismay, the new kid was seated directly beside me.

For reasons I couldn't fathom, he continuously gave me a creepy stare and proceeded to say "Hey" to me over and over again. I said "Hi" back every once in a while until it got annoying and I eventually managed to ignore him. Just before I was about to burst, I saw Ruby get out of the lunch line and, to my advantage, sit right across from me.

"You wanted to talk?" I asked, sarcastically, taking a sip of my water.

"Yes," she said, almost sounding official. "What's up with that guy you were walking to school with today?" she finished, though she went from official to sassy which I found quite infuriating. Almost more so than the new boy continuously trying to get my attention.

"Who?" I asked, trying to play dumb. "Oh, you mean Duke?" I said, almost teasingly. I wasn't sure why, but I found this whole situation somehow extremely entertaining.

"I guess," she said with a slight sigh. She began to eat some of her steak delicately, making me envy her a little more. She was both gorgeous and a prettier eater then I was.

"Oh, I know Duke. He's one of the butterflies, right?" the new kid said with food in his mouth. *That's revolting*, I thought, *at least I'm not as messy an eater as him.*

"Yeah, how do you know him? More importantly, how do you know about the butterflies?" I asked, inquisitively but also slightly concerned. I thought Cy, Blaze, and I were some of the few people who knew about them.

By now, Cy was sitting next to Ruby, and Blaze was next to me. Ruby's face was priceless as Bow sat down next to her.

"I met him in the woods a couple nights ago when I was hunting," he said, slightly trailing off. "Everyone knows about the butterflies," he added, still talking with food in his mouth. The very sight of it made my skin prickle up with goose bumps.

"Really?" I asked, amazed. *And here I am, thinking I'm so special for knowing something no one else does*, I scowled.

"I don't know about them," Ruby said, looking clueless as she set down her steak. It seemed she had paused her eating out of worry, which was exactly the reaction I was hoping for.

"It's kind of a long story," Blaze said, looking expressionless as he gulped down his water as if he were dying of thirst.

"Either way, you shouldn't hang out with him if you're annoying," I said, trying to imply something to Ruby though she didn't seem to understand. Cy, to my surprise and Phantom's amusement, gulped. *You're not the annoying one*, I thought to myself, wondering why she seemed to think so little of herself.

"Why?" Ruby asked, looking blankly at me. *Do you really not know?* I couldn't help but wonder, laughingly.

"He's killed a werewolf before, you know," I said, hoping this time she would figure it out on her own. Her expression turned from talking boys to talking killers as I began chomping down on my steak, finally satisfied that I had gotten a reaction.

"I've killed a werewolf before," the new boy said. "Nothing new," he finished, looking at a chunk of raw meat that he had been tossing around in his hands, staining them red with blood. He looked at all of us as if we were crazy. "Oh please! Like you've never killed someone," he simply laughed at us, almost disrespectfully.

"I've killed deer, but that's not the same. I don't even think I could work up the courage to kill one of my own kind!" I argued, pausing my eating. This topic seemed too serious to continue chomping away.

"Oh you will..." he mumbled under his breath so quietly that I could barely understand what he'd said. It was so quiet, in fact, that I wanted to make sure that was what he'd actually said.

"Excuse me?" I asked, though it didn't seem to get a reaction out of him. "What did you say?" I said, feeling the need to yell. My disruptive behavior was causing many of the wolves around us to look at our table, wondering what was wrong with us.

"What?" He asked innocently, obviously trying to change the subject, though still not answering my question.

"I said, 'what did you say'?" getting a little closer to his face and staring competitively into his eyes hoping he would find me intimidating.

"When?" he asked with a sly smirk as he took another bite of his steak.

"After I was done talking you mumbled something!" I said, reassuring him that he wasn't going to get off that easy.

"I don't know what you're talking about," he said simply, though I could tell he was obviously bluffing by the grin on his face.

"What did you say?" I asked, attempting to remain calm though it didn't seem to be working.

"I don't know," he said, though he also seemed to be trying to remain calm for some reason.

"How can you not know what you said?" I yelled, suddenly wondering why none of the teachers had tried to stop our argument. *I guess they think it's funny,* I thought to myself, which kind of calmed me down a little.

"Do you mind?" the new kid stood up and yelled at the countless number of people looking in our general direction. "I'm trying to have a friendly conversation here!" he said sarcastically, pointing accusingly down at me. Everyone quickly scrambled back to doing whatever they were doing before and finally stopped staring. "Geez! You people here are so rude!" he said, sitting back down, beginning to gobble up the rest of his food.

When he was done eating, I grabbed him by his collar. Again I was feeling an odd surge of rage pumping through my blood. "What did you say?" I said through clenched teeth. I could tell by the fear in his eyes that he knew I was serious.

Once again, everyone was staring at our table, looking just as scared as the new kid. It wasn't until I noticed what was actually happening that I realized I was acting crazy. I let go of his shirt, sat back down, and began to calm myself.

"Sorry," I said, attempting to apologize. "I guess I just haven't been myself since my mom died," I finished, trying to sound as sincere as I possible could. The fear in his eyes began to fade as if he understood what was happening to me.

"Still so sure you wouldn't hurt any of us?" Blaze asked with a wicked grin.

"I never said I wouldn't hurt one of us," I said, becoming my old, sarcastic self. "I just said I wouldn't kill my own kind. There's a difference," I explained.

"Who, exactly, would you hurt?" Bow asked, sounding half worried and half curious.

"Are you really going to ask me that question, Bocepheus?" I said, rolling my eyes. "You do realize that if I ever see you outside of school, it's going to be very difficult for me not to hunt you down," I said, wondering to myself whether or not I actually meant it.

He gulped and asked, "Why?" To my surprise, he looked baffled and as if he truly believed I was being serious.

"Because you're annoying," Ruby said, though I wasn't sure that's what I would have said. Cy sat quietly, eating her lunch. *I hope she doesn't feel left out,* I thought. This didn't necessarily seem to be Cyprus's 'crowd'.

"So anyways, I wouldn't hang out with him unless you don't mind possibly dying." I said, directing my attention back over to Ruby. What I had said came out kind of wrong, but I guess it worked. However, my attempt to scare her away had miserably failed.

If only I had been able to scare her off a little better, so many heartbreaks could have been avoided.

The Novus Proprius Chronicles

Chapter 10

Once lunch came to an end, we all headed back to the classroom, dreading the fact that we would have to actually learn now. As we all sat, lazily in our chairs, our bellies full and our eyes heavy, Gigi began to lecture us about how loud we'd been at lunch.

When I could no longer stand the annoyingly incessant pokes my back was receiving from the new kid, I turned around and yelled, "Do you mind?"

"Do you mind? You just interrupted the teacher!" he said, pointing at Ms. Gigi who simply rolled her eyes like a teenager, ignoring us completely.

"Okay kids. Now that we're done talking about that, I expect better behavior tomorrow," she said, looking at the five of us. She glanced at the new kid, saying, "Do you think you could, by any chance, stop poking Zaina's back for a few seconds and introduce yourself, new kid?" He simply sighed in annoyance.

"Can I wait until tomorrow?" he said, rubbing his eyes, trying to get around the fact of having to introduce himself.

"No!" Gigi yelled, making it visible that her patience was

all but used up.

"Fine then," he said, standing up lazily. There was something about him that made me believe he would have a rather odd name. "My name," he began, either pausing for effect or still trying to avoid his name, "is Phantom," he finished, taking a bow. I knew it, I thought. My instincts were always correct when it came to names.

"No it's not!" Ruby exclaimed, staring in disbelief. *Why is everything so hard for you to believe?* I thought to myself.

"What's wrong princess? Did you just now realize that not everyone is named after a gem?" he said, looking annoyed. "Anyways, I'd still like to be called 'new kid' if that's alright. It makes me feel special," he smirked almost wickedly, sitting back down in his chair.

For a split second, I thought I saw small fangs. Not like Duke's, however. They didn't seem to hang out of his mouth but they were there! I guess he noticed I noticed so he stopped smiling for a moment, pausing. When he smiled a second time, they weren't there. If it weren't for his immediate reaction to my stare, I would have thought it was all just a figment of my imagination.

"So, Phantom, how did you get here?" Gigi asked, though it almost didn't seem like a question. She seemed to address him as if he'd lived here all his life.

"I took a boat," he said simply. Suddenly, I noticed his bluish white eyes turn whiter. I glanced out the window to see why, and I noticed that he could see the blob also. However, like Ms. Gigi, he was about to refrain from looking at is, whereas I couldn't.

"What's a boat?" Cy asked, cocking her head to the side. *No! No more questions! Why did Cy ask some many questions?* I screamed inside my head.

"It's a thing that sits on water," he said, trailing off, either not knowing how to explain it or not wanting to.

"What's up with your eyes?" Ruby said, wrinkling up her nose.

"Well, my Dad was a werewolf but my mom was something called a witch," he said, causing Gigi's eyes to widen. Phantom simply stood there, grinning wickedly.

"What? I though," she paused, "I thought they were all dead," she said, though her reaction seem a little too fake. Almost as if she wasn't surprised.

"Oh no, they're all over the world," he said, still grinning wickedly as if all of this was simply a game.

"Okay look; I really don't care. Can we just learn what we're supposed to and go home?" I yelled, feeling another flash of anger. Phantom peered over at me, though he didn't look surprised by my anger. In fact, he simply laughed, looking away.

Since we didn't have much time left after Phantom was finally done talking, Ms. Gigi simply let us talk until the end of class. We discussed human school a little at first, but seeing as no one was paying attention she simply quit trying. As we call chit-chatted with one another, she sometimes interfered when I had an 'anger moment' and said something mean. At one point, I called Ruby 'idiot red' and Gigi told me that she wanted to talk to my dad later that night because she wasn't sure why I was acting this way. To make matters worse, she put me in time out as if I were a child.

"So, it's Zaina, right?" Phantom questioned, walking over to wear I was sitting in the back by myself. I sat, slouched back, looking angrily at everyone in the room. I couldn't help but wish I was at home, curled up by the fire like I always wanted to be when I was having a rough day.

"Yup," I said emotionlessly. *When can I just go home?* I thought to myself, angrily.

"Phantom," I could hear Gigi scold from across the room. "Get away from her. She's not supposed to be talking to anybody." The class got awkwardly quiet; so quiet I could almost hear my own heart beat. It seemed none of us really knew how to react.

"You said she couldn't talk to us, but you never told us that we couldn't talk to her," Phantom replied as if he were her long-lost, stubborn son who never did anything he was told.

"Oh well," she mumbled. "Zaina, you can walk around now." I'd heard what she said, though I didn't move.

There was something about my anger this time that made it seem to last. It was like I was a chipmunk and Gigi was the wolf. I felt defensive, like I needed to shield myself off from the rest of the world because they might hurt me. I felt like I wanted revenge against her because something inside of me just made me want to hurt everyone who touched me, including her. Well, everyone except—

I was dazed, staring at the blob which looked closer then

before, when I heard Gigi say, "Zaina, dear?" I think she could tell there was something wrong with me but simply didn't know how to ask me if I was alright.

"I'm fine." I said, standing up out of my chair and then sitting back down. "There, I got out of my chair. Happy now?" I asked without any emotion. There was something about the way I was acting that kind of reminded me of how Blaze always acted. Was it the emptiness of losing a parent that made us so similar in this situation?

Ms. Gigi looked away, almost seeming concerned as she began to rub her temples. Phantom, seeing that this wasn't a good time to talk to me, of course continued to talk. *This guy just doesn't quit,* I thought to myself.

"So how well do you know Duke?" he asked, pulling the pendant I'd somehow ended up wearing off my neck and looking it over eagerly; almost as if he'd recognized it.

"Not that good," I said simply, forgetting the necklace. "I only met him yesterday," I finished, laying my head down on the desk.

"Then how do you know that he killed one of us before?" He asked, seeming a little too curious for his own good.

"He told me," I said, feeling annoyed and rolling my eyes.

"Really? I had to get to know him for a while before he told me something that important," he said, looking at me curiously, again. "What else has he told you?" *You said you just met him the other night,* I thought to myself, suspiciously.

"Nothing," I said as I stood up and walked to the door. Phantom sat in his chair, looking dazed and wondering why everyone was leaving. Eventually he figured out that the bell had run and that it was time to go home.

As I walked out of the school, I was surprised to see Duke waiting outside of the school for me. When Ruby saw where I was going, she definitely was not thinking of the information I had told her at lunch today, and decided to follow me.

"OMG!" she shrieked. "Are you Duke?" Ruby said, sounding all too excited. Duke's face began to twist into a face that reminded me of the reaction someone has when they hear nails down a chalk board for the first time.

"Um yeah," he said, shooting me an accusing look. "I

can see I have a fan club now," he said, sounding annoyed by the attention.

"Don't blame me," I said defensively. "Idiot Red here has been following me around like a puppy dog all morning trying to find out more about you," I finished, pointing at her, feeling quite annoyed.

"Idiot Red?" he asked, seeming amused.

"Okay. That's like seriously hurtful," Ruby said, pouting with her arms crossed. Just the sound of her voice was enough to drive me mad at this point.

"Yeah, whatever," I said, as I began walking toward the woods.

"Wait, I want you to say you're sorry!" Ruby said, still pouting. Duke stayed out of the conversation, watching in amusement from afar.

"Sorry," I said, emotionlessly. The rage pumping inside my blood was beginning to boil now.

"Say it like you mean it!" she yelled, running after, looking for an apology she wasn't going to get.

"Remember what I said at lunch today?" I asked, about

to explode from pent up anger.

"You said a lot of things," she said, twirling her hair around her fingers.

"You make me crazy," I said, trying my best to keep control of my emotions.

"Oh, you mean about hurting us when we're not in school?" she said as if she had done nothing wrong.

"Yes, so keep that in mind," I said, turning back around and walking towards the woods again. By the time I thought I was away, I noticed she had continued to follow me.

"No really. Say it like you mean it. I won't leave till you do," I heard her say. Those were the last words I heard before I completely lost it, my humanity hanging by a string.

I couldn't remember much. I could remember Duke running in the other direction, probably to get my dad. However, as he ran, I attacked. I turned into my wolf form, only unlike my usual self, I could feel my hair spike up with rage. The look on Ruby's face made me feel like the most hated, ugly beast on the island and because of her condescending looks, I felt the need to lash out even more. I suddenly could no longer control my actions, and I was driven by pure rage.

The next few moments were strange; almost as if they were in slow motion. I remember her helpless screams and my nails digging into her side. Somehow, my claws had grown an inch thicker and longer from all the rage I was feeling. I also noticed that a large gash had formed down her cheek, though I couldn't remember causing it myself.

I suddenly stopped, realizing what I'd done. And for a moment, I felt bad. She couldn't help her personality. I, however, could help my rage if I'd really wanted to. As I backed off for split-second I thought she realized what was going on. She could tell what I was feeling; I could tell by the look in her eyes. I could also tell she knew something, I just needed to find out what it was.

Before I could ask, she yelled, "You freak!" The sympathy I felt was replaced with hatred once again. Soon, I was getting ready to attack again when someone held me back.

Duke

I was really surprised to see Zaina so...mad. I really hadn't expected her to lunge herself at Ruby, who had obviously just been searching for an apology in all the wrong places. The first thing that came to my mind when she first attacked was her dad. If anyone could stop her it was her own father, right?

As I ran in the woods I could hear Ruby, or 'Idiot Red' as Rusty called her, screaming. I think at this point Rusty had enough rage in her to attack the entire island. However, I couldn't figure out why she was so angry. This was something they didn't warn me about.

By the time I was at their cave, I could still hear screaming. I ran over half expecting her dad to come running out as well, but no. He was just sitting there reading something by the fire as if he didn't hear anything.

"Oh hey, Duke. Where's Zaina?" He asked as if she wasn't concerned at all.

"She's attacking a girl in her class! Can't you hear the poor girl screaming?" I yelled, pointing in their direction, now panicking.

"Oh that? Yeah, well guess she's going to learn sooner than I thought she would," he said, almost joyfully before continuing to read.

"Is this about that thing you told me earlier?" I asked, though I knew I had to hurry; the screaming still hadn't stopped.

"Yep," he said, smiling wickedly, putting his book in his lap.

"Don't you want to go stop her?" I yelled, looking around for a weapon just in case Rusty was unstoppable.

"No, this is how it is supposed to happen. Looks like Ms. Gigi has done her job," he said, staring into the fire in disbelief yet he somehow seemed happy.

"Fine. If you won't stop her I will," I said angrily. Before I began running back to Zaina and Ruby, I noticed him roll his eyes. "I'm not about to let an innocent girl die, no matter what the prophecies say," I said, stubbornly.

I was running toward the forest, again. For a moment, there was silence though it was broken when I heard Ruby scream something. At first I couldn't hear what she said, but then I heard Zaina scream something back incoherently. I was close enough to hear this time. Ruby had called Zaina a freak, not making the situation any better.

By the time I was close enough to see what was going

on, I could see that Ruby calling Zaina a freak was not the best move. *You think this girl would learn to keep her mouth shut,* I thought, in Zaina's defense. As Rusty went to lunge again, I was close enough to grab her and keep her from attacking.

Zaina

"Zaina. You don't want to do this," I heard a boy much younger than me say. Why was he holding me back? Who was he? And why was he calling me Zaina? *Why am I fuzzy?* I thought frantically. "It's me, Duke," he said, reassuringly.

"Zaina?" I questioned, but then it clicked. I suddenly turned back into my human form and said, "I...got a little lost." When I was back to myself, I ran over to Ruby who was shaking so hard I thought she had hypothermia. I wasn't quite sure how she'd gotten so far away.

"Stay away, savage!" she shrieked, looking at Duke with pleading eyes as if to try and get him to get me away from her.

"Oh my gosh Ruby! I am so sorry!" I sobbed. Something inside me told me that she would never trust me again, though I couldn't blame her.

"Get away from me!" she yelled once more, trying to get up only to miserably fail. I helped her to her feet even though something inside me told me that she would rather have had Duke help her up.

"Ruby, I really am sorry!" I said, though I knew 'sorry' wasn't going to cut it.

I wasn't mad that she was trying to get away from me. After all I had cut her face, which was bleeding out scarlet colored blood. Not only that, but there was also a huge gash, almost a hole somehow, in her side. You could see where my claws, that were once nails, had cut through her flesh like butter.

She once again tried running away. Duke and I both held her up as she began to fall.

"Ruby, you can't go home. You need to go to the doctor on the island," Duke said, calmingly. "You guys do have a doctor right?" he asked, looking at me.

"No, we don't. People fend for themselves here," I said sadly.

"Then what," Ruby began, spitting out blood, "what do you expect me to do? Just bleed out and die?" she said, frantically.

I suddenly heard a branch snap behind me, and for a second I thought it might be Gizmo. However, as I turned around I noticed it was, well, I wasn't sure who it was.

"Ruby!" the woman almost seemed to squawk as she ran over and started hugging the girl and sobbing. I'd never seen her before on the island, which was odd. Everyone knew everyone; that's just how it was on the island.

"Who are you?" I asked, for some reason starting to feel protective over Ruby. The only explanation I could come up with was my guilt making me feel like I owed her something.

"I'm Blair, Ruby's sister. I heard her screaming and saw that she was being attacked by something, but I think it ran away," She said, looking in the direction Duke had come from.

"No, I don't think it ran," Duke said, possibly trying to find out if she'd seen my face.

"No really. It ran away. I saw it," she said, matter-of-factly. I didn't think there was any way of change her mind; she seemed very certain of what she'd seen.

"I thought I hurt her," I said, innocently, feeling truly

baffled.

"No, you were trying to fight it," she said, reassuringly. "But it ran away! Trust me, I saw it run," She argued, leaving the one simple, yet unexplainable question: if I didn't hurt her, who did?

Chapter 11

"It's just not possible for me not to have hurt her. I saw it. I *did* it for crying out loud!" I argued as Duke and I were watching Blair tend to her helpless sister's open wounds from a distance. As I was staring in disbelief, she looked over and gave me an overprotective glare. Had she heard what I just said?

"Then how do you explain Blair seeing that thing run in the other direction?" Duke asked, trying to reason with me; unfortunately with no success.

As I gazed at the two sisters, trying to figure out what had happened, I realized something. Blair had that same jewelry box look to her that Ruby did. They both had fine features, both very elegant in the way their faces were structured. They all in all looked like princesses, and everyone knew they were to be treated as such as well. However, there was something about Blair that seemed a little darker, almost evil. It could have just been due to the dark brown, almost black hair she had in comparison to Ruby's fair, ginger hair, though there was something off about Blair. I could feel it.

"I don't know. Maybe," I began, though I began to stutter the words, "I don't know" repeatedly. I was suddenly comforted by the fact that I was starting to forget what really happened.

"Maybe what?" Duke looked at me curiously. There was always something about him that I didn't get. Just that fact that he always seemed more interested in what I thought than anything else. I wasn't sure why he thought I was so interesting or special.

"I don't know. Maybe—maybe something was trying to trick us?" I asked. Though I wanted it to sound like I was suggesting this statement, it came out more as a question.

"I guess," he hesitated for a moment, as if he were thinking about what I just said. "I guess it could be possible," he finished, with a slight shrug of his shoulders.

Then something caught his eye. The way he was acting made it seem as if he was going to say something. Something important, but I could tell that he just couldn't bring himself to do so. Or perhaps he wasn't sure how to word it. What was he not telling me?

As Duke and I continued to ponder reasons for the strange attack, he suddenly stopped talking mid-sentence. I followed his line of sight and realized what had caught his attention. I looked around to see if other people had noticed it as well, and judging by their baffled looking faces, they had. The sight of it even caused Blair to stop tending to her sister's wounds for a moment to gawk at the strange phenomena above us.

It was like nothing I had ever seen. What looked like ten at first soon became fifty butterflies flying in the sky, carrying big boxes that I had never seen before. All the people gathered around to see if Ruby was okay suddenly scattered to where they thought the butterflies might land. Most of them had never even seen the butterflies before and were suddenly awestruck, thinking the world was ending.

I ran away from Blair and Ruby, not even paying attention to them. Suddenly, the health of Idiot Red was completely beside the point. I was too curious to find out what was in those boxes to care what had happened during the attack and if Ruby would even survive. *I'm sure she'll be fine,* my insensitive mind told myself.

"Zaina, wait up!" Duke was yelling from behind me. Just then I realized that not only my nails had grown longer, but my stride as well. I also noticed that my attention span was growing increasingly short as I got mad.

I slowed down to walk, although Duke was still having trouble keeping up. By now, I felt like I had a fire growing inside of me. It was odd; I felt like if I didn't run my anger out, I would just burst.

What was happening to me? The sudden changes in behavior seemed to be the biggest problem, though little things were bothering me, too. I suddenly felt like I didn't care enough to know if those around me were okay, or even if Ruby would live after my attack. It was like I was becoming more of an animal than anything else. I felt like my humanity was struggling to keep the beast inside from bursting out of my skin. I couldn't help but feel like there was no where for me to hide.

"Sorry, I'm just so curious," I said, though I'd planned to make up a better excuse. As we got close enough to see what was going on, we peered through the woods, hoping not to be seen. As we stood there, snooping, I heard someone suddenly sneaking up on us from behind.

I found it quite odd how I could suddenly hear better, too. I heard anything from the rustling in the trees from the amber colored leaves, to the small chipmunks in the bushes. I could almost hear the faintest heartbeat of something near by. However, it was so faint I could barely tell if it was mine or even Duke's for that matter. But then I realized that the person sneaking up on us didn't have a heartbeat.

"Man, you caught me," I heard Phantom say as I swung around as fast as I could. The way he said it was playful and a little mocking though I was just glad it was someone I knew behind us.

The look on Phantom's face made me feel like he was trying to think of something to say, he just didn't know what—or even how. *What is wrong with you people?* I asked myself. I felt like I was behind bars and they had figured out something I wasn't supposed to know. *What are you people not telling me?* I screamed in my head.

By now Duke had turned around too. "So," he said, pausing again, only this time he seemed to be searching for the right words. "How's your hearing?" His face turned into a sly smirk as if he knew all the answers to the questions in my life.

Duke suddenly seemed to notice my frustration bubbling up inside me and before I could lunge like I did before, he was able to hold me back. I found that my strength was becoming more fragile. Like I could only use it so long before it felt like my body was going to give up; as if my body couldn't handle the strength it suddenly seemed to possess.

"Hold it. No need to get physical here." He rolled his eyes in a sarcastic way. "I haven't gone home yet, and you are still on 'school property' if you haven't stepped foot into your own cave. By which I mean that there is no fighting allowed on school grounds," he said mockingly. His strange sarcasm made me calm down, oddly enough. It was true, however. Those were almost the exact words that were in the newsletter. *I wonder how he got one,* I thought, suspiciously.

"Sorry, I," I began, though this time I hesitated. "Today's been pretty awful," I finished. He looked back to where Ruby and Blair were sitting in the middle of the woods. You couldn't see them from here, but I think he could sense that they were there.

"Oh yeah, I heard," he said, laughing a slight wicked laugh. Was Phantom always this cold?

"Heard? How or who did you hear from?" Duke asked,

looking concerned, though a slight bit of annoyance was also detectable.

"Let's just say that when people heard Ruby scream, they could only imagine the worst," he said as he again hesitated, only this time he seemed to be looking for more amusing words. "I mean, granted she screams at everything that moves, literally, but no one could mistake that kind of a scream." This time he hesitated and looked over at Duke, as if to try and tell him something. Then he smirked and continued. "Yeah, you're like the town hero now; saving Ruby and everything," he finished, shrugging.

"What?" Duke and I both said at the same time, making us look at each other awkwardly. Situations like that always made me feel awkward.

"Well, you should have known that when people hear screaming, everyone wants to know what is happening—especially in a small place like this," he said, ending the sentence so softly I could barely hear him.

"What do you mean?" I was, for some reason, having trouble shutting my mouth. All the questions in my head were beginning to spill over like a pot left on the stove for too long.

"What I mean is, when they heard the screaming everyone went to see what was going on." Once again, he hesitated. "Now, I know that the others may have seen something else attack Ruby, but I didn't. I saw you," he said with the slightest bit of fear detectable in his voice. There was still something he wasn't telling me; I could sense it. "I also know about what's been happening to you; the mood swings and all," he said, though just the sound of hope made it impossible for me to let him finish.

"So what? Am I bipolar or something?" I asked, spitting out the first few words that came to my mind; he simply laughed as if I should have known better.

"Not necessarily. You see, that's why I was getting on your nerves earlier. Just wanted to see how you would react," he chuckled, but soon stopped when he saw my face. I believe he was beginning to pick up on the fact that I didn't find this at all as amusing as he found it.

Suddenly, an angry, deep yet still feminine voice that sounded so furious it could shatter glass yelled "Tom" from behind us, causing all three of us to jump.

"One second," he said, putting his index finger up and whispering just loud enough for us to hear him. "Coming, Mom," he said, his eyes displaying annoyance, his tone displaying caution.

"Mom, huh?" I asked, stopping his in his tracks. "Maybe she would like to know how you behave at school," I said, wanting my statement to sound like a threat though it just ended sounding like a question.

This time it really did sound like I was teasing him for once. There was something about the look on his face that made me perk up a little more, and want to tell his mom. The look clearly said 'Please don't! She'll kill me!' which I found oddly enough quite amusing.

"TOM!" She yelled once more when realizing he was no longer walking in her general direction. His mom simply sounded mean spirited.

Hearing his mother speak to him like that made me feel rather awful; not all of us have—or had—loving parents like I did. Maybe there was a reason why he was a showoff at school. Maybe he simply longed for attention at school because he didn't get it at home.

"She's kidding," Duke said, thinking he'd noticed it too. Although, to my knowledge, they hadn't really known each other for that long, it seemed like they already knew each other down to the core, which I found quite odd.

"Sure she is," he said, almost seeming to chuckle a little due to nerves, running to try and get to where his mom was standing, her foot tapping angrily on the ground.

Even from a distance, you could tell she was yelling at him. There was something about the way that she talked that seemed to give it away—maybe it was the fact that her loose, high bun bobbed up and down while she yelled. The saddest part of all was seeing a young man like Phantom crouch down as the angry women raised her hand—he was scared of her. And I hated seeing that. Behavior such as that was usually never tolerated, but I guess their customs were different from where they came.

I hadn't known him for too long, but I had always thought of him as one of the tough guys that you didn't mess with because they looked like they would tear your eyes out. It was odd, feeling sympathy for a guy like him. Up until this point I had loathed him, though now there was only pity in my heart.

There was also something about Phantom that kind of reminded me of a memory. It wasn't clear, but distant. Like you knew it was there, but it wasn't. It felt like I was trying to sweep away dirt in the woods. Something that seemed impossible to get to.

Phantom ran over to us again. "Okay, my mom saw me talking to you guys and wants to meet you," he said, looking like he had just come out of a torture chamber. "Please don't tell her. She really *will* beat me," he said, for the first time not sounding sarcastic. I was shocked to hear that. I think he could tell by the look on my face that I wouldn't and gestured us to move forward.

We walked out onto a big, open field that seemed to stretch for miles. At the end of the countless miles was the ocean. It had always seemed so beautiful with its waves, the sound of soft sweet humming and then the sand; it wasn't hard and rough on the bottoms of my feet like the woods. Such a surface was comfortable and caused a longing in a wolf's heart to stay there forever and simply never leave.

The grass was tall and waved back and forth, as if welcoming us. As I walked over to Phantom's mom, barefooted in shorts and a black tank top that said 'Beware! I bite!' in red letters, the grass's dew seemed to cover my legs as if trying to create an impenetrable stocking to protect me from anything. We were getting closer and closer to Phantom's mom, which caused the hair on my arms to stand up.

Everything about that woman screamed vicious, mean, evil, and cruel. I realized that her hair wasn't black, it was a midnight blue, causing her to seem a little more eerie. Never in my life had I seen a werewolf with blue hair—as black as it may look. Her differences were a bit terrifying. I'd never seen anyone who looked even remotely like her. Her hollowed out cheek bones matched her almost skeletal body which was covered head to toe with clothing as if skin was an unwelcoming object of the body no one should see. Her eyes were black and deep, as if she didn't have the capability to own a soul. She had a menacing presence that made you want to run away and hide. How Phantom had put up with this woman for so many years completely baffled me.

She stood there, judging Duke and I as she looked us both up and down twice—as if she were scanning us to see how special we were. As we'd walked over to meet this horrific looking woman, Duke had let go of my arms, but I could tell by the way he was standing, the direction, that he was ready to tackle me down if needed. *That's what friends are for, right?* I asked myself. It was sad to think that I needed someone ready to hold me back from attacking someone.

I reached my hand out as if to shake her hand and said, "Hi, my name is Zaina," with a smile. I pulled my hand back awkwardly when I saw her face turn from displeased to utter disgust by the idea of touching my hand. However, eventually there was some kind of relief in her eyes that was both tragic and menacing. It was almost as if a shield had been broken, somehow.

To my surprise, she suddenly reached out her own hand, as if to gesture to shake mine. "I thought you looked familiar. My name is…well, you can call me Tom's mom," she said, looking down at me over her hooked nose.

We shook hands formally as I looked over at Phantom and asked, "Tom?" His mom looked startled at the question, though I was merely confused. *I thought his name was Phantom,* I thought to myself.

"Tom—right there," she said, pointing at Phantom who looked like a poor, lost, kicked puppy.

"I thought," Phantom, or Tom, in this case gave me a

warning glare. "Oh sorry, I keep thinking your name is… well, not Tom. You remind me of someone…else," I stuttered, wondering if his mother could tell I was lying. By the looks of it, I wasn't sure she could.

"Hi, I'm Duke," he said, cheerfully reaching out a hand. He, however, didn't get a friendly shake like I did. *What is her problem?* I asked myself. After he drew his hand back, he asked, "So, what's in the boxes?" I could tell this wasn't going to go anywhere. It seemed that there was something about me that she thought was exceptionally average.

"Duke," I said, pointing to Phantom who had left shortly after he had seen his mother's face light up after meeting me—like he realized it too, and seemed offended. What was it though? "Just go talk to Tom," I finished, and judging by Tom's mother's face, she liked my assertiveness.

Then I wondered why everyone was changing their names. I could understand why the butterflies would change their name; I could see them striking the top of the list when it comes to murder suspects—but a werewolf?

"Fine, whatever," he said angrily, walking over to Phantom who was now examining a box that said 'Tom's stuff.

Do not enter.'

"I'm sorry about him," I said, directing my attention back to his mother who was staring at Phantom. The look she gave him was one that usually made it feel like your neck was on fire. "He can be pretty nosey sometimes. Do you think I could call you something other than Tom's mom?" I asked as politely as I could. I attempted at 'sweet-talking' Phantom's mom merely because Duke wasn't the only one who was curious about those boxes.

"You can call me Ellen," she said, smiling for once; her dark demon eyes glaring down at me.

"Okay, Ellen," I said, Ellen seeming pleased, like she'd just discovered something that she knew, but then again didn't. "So, hate to be nosey myself, but what is in the boxes?" I asked, hoping I hadn't just ruined my chance at finding out the truth.

"Huh, I thought you would ask," she said, pausing—she seemed to do the same thing as Phantom. Like she knew more than she was telling and wanted to tell, but couldn't. "In the boxes is all our crap."

"You keep feces in boxes? That's disgusting!" I yelled,

utterly disgusted by that fact.

"No! It's not—it's—it's just—just something that we said back where we used to be. I meant we have all our stuff in the boxes," she said, seeming appalled by the very idea.

"Okay," I said, rolling my eyes. I was still kind of confused about the motivation behind calling things 'feces.' "Tom said you came by boat?" I asked, and she simply nodded. "So, where did you guys come from?" I, for some reason, thought she was going to give me that same look of disgust, but she seemed to give me a look of acceptance; almost as if she appreciated my curiosity whereas detested Duke's.

"Well, we moved from this little island called Hollings. It's basically the same as here, Meadows, only it had more of a variety of," she hesitated once more, "creatures," she finally finished.

"Oh," I said, feeling speechless. Before now, I didn't even know there were other islands. I thought this was the only one—I didn't even know this place was called Meadows! *That's pretty sad,* I thought, *I don't even know the name of my own island.*

"What kind of creatures?" I asked, feeling like a scientist at the brink of a new discovery. She was about to answer my question when Phantom came over, probably on purpose.

"Cyprus wants you," he said, not looking at Ellen who seemed utterly disgusted that her son had interrupted our conversation.

"What?" I asked, scanning the crowd for a bleach blonde. It was then that I saw the usual duo—a white haired girl and a black haired boy. It was funny how you could rarely find Cy without Blaze by her side. *And they say they don't like each other*, I thought. It was sad to think that everyone but Cy knew that Blaze was head over heals in love with her.

"Yeah, Cyprus is here. She saw the butterflies and came to see what was happening like everyone else. Literally everyone is here," he informed me, his eyes wide with excitement. I could have sworn he loved the attention of being the 'new kid.'

"Oh, okay," I said, starting to walk away, but then remembering Ellen. "It was nice meeting you," I said, after turning back to look at her. She gave me a friendly nod and sweet smile, but Phantom got an unnecessary frown that didn't say much of anything.

On the way over to were Cy and Blaze were standing, Phantom was talking to me with pure and obvious jealousy. "Looks like my mom really likes you," he began. "I wouldn't happen to know why," he finished, mumbling quietly, but just loud enough for me to hear and get on my nerves.

"I guess," I shrugged, not really caring. I stopped, turned and waited a moment. When I stopped, he stopped as if he were expecting me to do so. I wanted to ask him, but I wasn't sure how he would react.

"Just ask, I know you want to," he said, making me wonder if he somehow read my mind or if my expression had told the story.

"Your mom doesn't treat you right, does she?" I asked, noticing at that moment, a glimpse of fangs in the corner of his mouth, just like I had at school—or were those, again, just a figment of my imagination? Now they seemed to be gone as he calmed down. It was strange. It seemed that every time I got mad, I would find someone to blame or take my anger out on, but he seemed to sprout fangs.

"Let's just say, she wishes I were someone else," he said, emotionlessly. I hadn't known Phantom for more than a day, and I had only seen him as a stubborn blonde boy who had a knack for annoying just about everyone.

However, there was something about him now that made me feel sorry for him. Then there was another feeling. A feeling of guilt, sweet yet sinister at the same time. I felt like I had done something myself. Something that I couldn't remember, but if I did I would never be able to forgive myself. As much as I tried to push through the barriers that separated the lie from reality, the truth would not come. There was something there that wouldn't allow me to remember. All this pounding at an invisible wall that possibly didn't even exist, just made my head hurt.

Phantom kept walking before I could ask him who his mother wished he were. Even if I would have gotten the chance to ask, I don't think he would have told me. That just seemed to be a 'Phantom thing' he would do. His pace quickened; whether it was to avoid the question or to avoid me in general I wasn't sure. By now we were standing next to Cy and Blaze.

"Oh my gosh! Look at all this stuff!" Cy said poking one

of the boxes with her index finger, staring in fascination.

"Yeah, very cool," I said, almost bitterly. "Did you see what I saw earlier?" I asked, her face changing from fascinated to worried.

She looked at me in concern and said, "What? The butterflies or Ruby?" I nodded as she mentioned 'Ruby' and she continued, "I guess. Anyways, whoever did that is either insane or has some serious anger issues!" she said, throwing her hands up in the air. *So she didn't see it either?* I asked myself. *Great, now my best friend thinks I'm a psychopath*, I told myself bitterly.

"I guess that answers my question," I said, turning around to see Duke standing behind me.

I felt a weird rush go to my head. Again I felt as if someone where trying to tap into my thoughts. Then I realized that I got the same feeling of wanting to protect my own thoughts only when Duke was looking into my eyes. Was it possible that the butterflies could read minds if they looked into one's eyes?

To test my new idea, I tried freeing my mind, to open up to him or whoever it was trying to read me. I thought, *If you're reading my mind, do a little dance.* This seemed quite ridiculous and amusing at the same time.

He laughed, as if hearing what I thought and indeed did a little dance with his arms, as if jogging in place. *That's both cool and creepy,* I thought to myself, thinking of all the times I'd thought something odd while around Duke.

"Excuse me Duke," I said, losing the smile and replacing it with a frown once more. "I'm sure my dad is wondering why I'm not home yet," I continued. "That is if he didn't come to see what was going on, too," I finished, mumbling. His face went blank and this time, when the rush came, it felt like something was wrong. There was something about his face that seemed to scare me a little. I wasn't scared of him, just of what he wasn't telling me.

"Wait, Zaina. Don't leave. What did you want to ask?" Cy said trying to stop me with no success. I could feel a mood swing coming on, so sudden it felt like heartburn.

"Nothing," I bluffed. "Really, it's nothing," I said, looking around at all of them. They were staring at me as if they were either guilty of something or as if I had a monkey sitting on my head that they had purposely put there themselves to make me look idiotic.

I fixed my gaze back on Cy. "Look, I'd love to stay and chat, but I really need to get home," I said. The look on her face was full of self-hatred. Something told me that she was just about ready to burst out crying; though Cy was often overly emotional, this seemed like something she wouldn't do. Ignoring her sorrowful eyes, however, I turned around and began walking towards my house.

I was just about to be swallowed up by the dense forest's edge when Cy hopelessly called out one more time. "Zaina, wait. Wait!" Her voice seemed to squeak a little at the end.

When I was sure no one could see me, I turned back and listened to their conversation. Looking at them, I could see Blaze holding Cy back the way Duke had held me back earlier. Lucky for me, my hearing had improved enough to the point where I could hear their voices. They were distant, like faded memories, but they were there.

"Just let her go. She needs to find out on her own," Duke said almost angrily, Blaze still holding her back. Instead of self-hatred, there was longing in her eyes; a type of longing to say something.

"Man, I knew you shouldn't have told her," Blaze said, also angrily, as Duke simply shook his head.

"You wanted to tell her! Okay? Not me!" Duke yelled, throwing his hands in the air. Tell me what? I thought as I stared at them.

"Please, Zee is my best friend. I can't keep lying to her!" Cy yelled, struggling to get away from Blaze's grip. So that had something to do with the whole thing. That made me start to wonder what else she and the others weren't telling me.

"See, that's the point. She needs to find out on her own. You read the prophesies; the future got messed up because you told her too much. Ember doesn't want that really happening," Phantom said, though he'd stayed out of the conversation until now. He seemed to be the only person who was trying to reason with her rather then just yell at her.

There was a certain yet untraceable harshness in his voice that made him sound more like her older brother then the annoying boy we had only known for a day. He suddenly seemed so much more mature, and more like a leader then he normally did. However, just as they were ignoring her pleas, she was ignoring theirs.

As they continued talking about things I had no clue about, a number of questions raced through my head. *Who was Ember?* I thought. *And, how am I supposed to do or find out anything if I don't even know something is happening, and people won't tell me?*

In the end, they decided to talk about it another time after Cy swore multiple times not to tell me anything that I wasn't supposed to find out. While Blaze, Cy, and Phantom sat around talking about school things, Duke sat and read a book.

I always thought how amazing it was to sit down and simply read. It seemed to take your mind off things. Just like the way water washes away dirt and soil, reading washes away sadness, grief, anger—even hatred.

I started heading home. As I walked, questions were being written in my mind. It seemed that every time I stepped on a branch, heard it snap, a new question would pop up. Just thinking about that fact that Cy had been lying to me made me start to wonder. Was our friendship even real? Was she really my friend? Or was she just another piece to the endless puzzle with so many different wrong answers, that it was basically impossible to find the right one.

I had arrived at my cave, only to find it empty. There was no fire going and the book that my dad would always read wasn't lying in the corner where it usually was. Of course I wasn't expecting to see my mom's book lying on the ground, even though something inside me ached to find it; to see it. Even just to touch it.

"Dad? You there?" I yelled, anxiously. This seemed to be what was written on Duke's face earlier. It was both frustration and misery. "Dad?" I shrieked, unsure of what to do. This uncertainty seemed to terrify me. I suddenly had no one; I felt completely alone.

Out of the corner of my eye, I caught a glimpse of pointed wings and I suddenly knew it was a butterfly. Seeing as they all seemed to look the same, yet somehow so extremely different, I was ready to pounce after evolving into my wolf form. My amber coat was shining in the setting sun, making me wonder how long I was actually gone.

"Zaina?" Now seeing that the butterfly was Byrd, I grew back into what Cy calls my 'human form.' I never really got why she said 'human form' when we were anything but human. Byrd didn't turn, however. Sometimes I wondered if she knew anything about the prophecies Duke and the other had talked about. She always seemed so innocent. Either she was a really good actress or she really didn't know anything.

"Byrd, where's my dad?" I asked, my tone was harsh, yet cracking because of fear. I had no idea what I should do because I'd never been in such a situation.

"Your dad, Richard?" she asked, and I simply nodded. "I have no clue," she finished, turning into her perfect yet worried self. I then noticed how most people looked like what they were named. There was just something about the name Byrd that made me think beautiful and free. Byrd fit the description with her long corkscrew black hair and then, even in her butterfly form, she still had a sense of beauty which most butterflies seemed to lack.

Suddenly, I found it hard to remember much. I did remember Byrd trying to catch and somehow stop me as I ran. However, I was too fast and slick and got away just before she was about to grab my arm. I wasn't sure where I was running to; all I knew was that I needed to get away.

I was surprised to see her not running after me. In fact, as I looked behind me, she seemed to be waving 'good bye' as I ran. Seeing as I really didn't care, I continued to run.

I didn't know where I was headed to. I was just running. As I did so, the branches whipped at my legs. My right leg shot pain up into my spine as I, for some reason, brushed by a branch that turned into a knife as I hit it. It dug into my leg, making it ooze out blood. The cut was deep but I didn't care. Although, the smell of my own blood was repulsive, and made me gag, I wasn't expecting to be surrounded by things that would, in turn, make me gag much, much more.

Despite the pain, my rage dared me to keep going. Somehow, I ended up in that same open field where I had been just a few minutes ago.

It seemed impossible. The long, thick grass that used to wave at you and greet you was now mere dead dirt. All it did now was portray a warning.

There were four graves where Cy, Blaze, Duke, and Phantom had been talking. One of the graves was dug open and the bones were scattered across the ground just like the dirt was scattered across the names of the deceased. I went up and moved the dirt aside. On three graves stood: Cyprus. Tom. Blaze.

Another rush went to my head. That most likely meant that the other grave was Duke's. I looked over at the dug up grave, only to find the bones missing. I felt something tap my shoulder. When I turned around, I saw Duke's bloody and moving corpse; the flesh rotting and falling off the bone right then and there. There was a foul smell lingering in the air as if it were made to ward people off. As if it was there only to keep people away so they wouldn't find out a secret; a secret only the dead could know and understand.

In his left hand, he was holding the book my mom had been reading shortly before she died. He handed it to me. As our hands touched, more flesh fell off, exposing both bone and more of the vulgar smell.

I took the book, and it seemed like something was telling me to look inside, so I did. On the cover, it said "All the times I've lied to you." I opened it to the first page. All it said was two words.

I'm sorry.

I closed it, suddenly shocked to hear a voice coming

from under the dirt of Cy's grave. I looked down and I could see her clawing her way out of the ground. Her hands are cut up, probably from digging.

As she clawed her way out, she said, "These are all the people you've killed." Her voice had never sounded so distant before. Instead of liveliness, her voice contained agony and for a while, it sounded like she was mocking me.

I didn't know how I couldn't have noticed the other graves, but they were there...now. Hundreds of them. Cy was pulling herself up and out of the grave by then. She had a small blade in her dirty, blood covered hand. Her hair was matted into brown braids whereas it normally was short and choppy silk.

Now the rest of the graves were slowly coming so life. There was my mom. My dad. Gigi. Everyone I knew, really. They all had knives in their hands and filthy dirt and blood tangling their hair just like Cy's.

Out of the corner of my eyes I saw a young girl standing by a tree looking out as if she were watching. I didn't know her, but there was something oddly familiar about her. Then I saw Blair in front of me.

Her knife seemed sharper than the rest. As she leaned over, she began carving something into my flesh. It was right below my ribcage on the left side. Like my legs, the cut burned. While she was cutting me, I found myself strangely paralyzed. My head was the only thing I could move. I looked over, only to see no one by the tree anymore, even though I could have sworn I had before.

As Blair was still cutting, Duke said, "You did this to me. You did this to all of us. We wouldn't tell you. Never!" He spat plainly. "I'm sorry." The last two words were as soft as a freshly washed blanket, but they still contained a certain degree of hatred for some reason. By now, Blair was done carving and everything went dark. For a moment or two, I thought I had died. The pain was unbearably real even after the light returned.

Chapter 12

I looked around, and suddenly realized it had all simply been a dream. The pain somehow continued to hurt. It wasn't until I actually looked that I noticed a real gash, It was odd. It was the shape of a tear drop. In my dream, Blair had even taken the time to fill it in. *How nice of her,* I thought mockingly. Unfortunately, I really didn't know how much of it actually was a dream. To me, if felt like an ongoing story.

I got up off the straw mattress that I had been laid on next to the fire that was sadly still dead. Despite the fact that the fire had, to my understanding, never been lit there were amber coals in the middle of it that made me wonder who else was here.

I felt a sudden heavy feeling in my head that made me unbearably dizzy. My arms felt heavy and sore, but that was the least I could say for my legs. They were cut up in multiple places and then there was the huge open wound that was still oozing out scarlet blood and yellow pus, despite the bandage that was wrapped around it. But those were the cuts that I had gotten from a dream. If it weren't for the claw-like branches and the moving corpses, I would have sworn that it was reality.

I walked out to find Ms. Gigi standing outside the cave as if she were waiting for me. As she looked over I thought, *Where's Duke?*

"Gigi?" My tone was cautious, yet curious. "What are you doing here?"

"Oh hello Zaina. Your father asked me to come pick you up today. How are you feeling?" she asked. She seemed worried as she glanced down at my torn up clothes and half shredded up legs.

I had always found it incredibly odd that teachers seemed so worried about you almost as if they were your parents, when they had no real right to worry or know how you were feeling. I also thought it was funny how Gigi would get mad at you for asking stupid questions. Yet, if you really thought about how stupid it was to ask someone 'how they are feeling' when their leg is gapping wide open, it seemed perfectly okay to be angry with her as well.

"I'm fine," I bluffed. "Where's my dad?" This time, my reply was unsteady. There was something about her face that made me think she was scared of me. Why I wouldn't know.

As I saw that look, I told myself that there was a lot of

things that everyone wasn't telling me and I'd do whatever I had to in order to find out what those things were. As I thought this, I remembered what Duke had said.

"You did this to me. You did this to all of us. I wouldn't tell you. Never." Just remembering the dream made me wonder if the dream was the future, or just a nightmare. Any way you choose to look at it, either one could be true.

"Um, he is—" The pause in her sentence seemed to drag on forever.

Was she looking for a lie or was her memory nearly erased too? I didn't see how my dad could possibly have had anything to do with saving the world. Was she afraid that I would go looking for him? "He won't be back for a while." She finally said. Now I felt like I was going to cry.

Was this karma? I had told Duke he was lucky for not having parents, but now that I didn't have any myself it just hurt. It felt like my heart was screaming. Bleeding from the inside out.

"Where is he?" I could feel my anger start to boil up inside me again, though it was the kind of anger that made me want to break down and cry.

"I—" she hesitated once more. She looked down at my once small and delicate nails that were now turning into thick heavy claws. They were ready to dig into fragile skin and tough bone if needed.

There was something odd about my claws this time. They were shiny. Like pearls. Until recently, they were just thick bone, but now they looked like solid rock. Not only solid, but unbreakable.

"I can't tell you," she stuttered. *Big mistake*, I thought as I evolved. My coat now looked like amber colored silk. My coat had never been this soft or even looked silky.

Right before I lunged at her, I thought for sure she was going to jump up the tree standing at her side. Then, I lunged. As I did so, my mind went blank. I couldn't feel my entire body. It felt like another bad dream. The type of dream where I stood up in the cloudbank watching and couldn't look away, much as I wanted to.

As much as I had wished, this wasn't a bad dream. As I had predicted, Gigi did try and climb up the tree. I was trying to tell myself that she didn't deserve to be attacked, yet I couldn't *stop* myself from attacking.

It felt like I had no control over my own body; like the animal inside me was starting to come out more and more. Before she could get away, I managed to catch her by her ankle. My five inch long claws went right through her ankle, as if it was nothing more than butter.

As I did so, she let out a scream that was louder than my own howl. Her scream actually scared me enough to the point to where I pulled my claws out. They were covered in a scarlet colored blood that had a different smell and texture than a werewolf's.

While her blood smelled abnormally sweet, mine would smell sour as poison. The density was thinner. Werewolf blood was almost like pudding. Plus, our blood is a darker red than hers. I wondered why she hadn't tried to run away. Though she had tried to climb the tree, running and dodging the attack seemed like a much better plan in my opinion.

Not only could I smell her blood, but I could also smell flesh—freshly ripped open. It reminded of my dream. Then Duke's bloody, still somehow moving corpse flashed in my mind.

Just like in my dream, he handed me the book. Somehow, I managed to take it, even though I was daydreaming. I opened the book to the first page, again just like in the dream. Inside the book, it said, "I change my mind. I'm not sorry." What did that mean? Until now, I had only seen dreams as random, meaningless images, but now I wasn't so sure.

"Talk," I said, my voice sharp as my claws as I helped her down from the tree and onto the ground where she began to tend to her wound.

How I had said that reminded me of how Blair had said she was doing this for her sister, because I had hurt her. Then I realized that I hadn't remembered that part of my dream until just that moment. *How odd*, I thought to myself. Then the smell from my dream came back to me—the boiling blood and rotting flesh.

All this made me gag. It seemed that the more I thought about my dream, the more I felt sick. After gagging multiple times, and almost throwing up once, I returned to my normal self, if there was such a thing. Then, in the corner of my eye I saw the blob as I usually did when something weird was happening to me, I was zoning out, or I was supposed to be paying attention to something. Then, I noticed that

Gigi had of course been talking the whole time while I was, not surprisingly, zoning out.

"Wait, hold on what?" I asked, focusing my attention back on Gigi but the blob was still there, making it increasingly difficult to keep my attention on her.

"I said, 'can I tell you after school some time?' It's about time for everyone to be arriving at school right now and I don't want to be late…sort of," She supposedly repeated. The look on her face told me that she had said something else, but my now softhearted self felt bad for her. She did, after all have a huge gash in her ankle.

On our way to school, Gigi kept limping. That was another fact about her that made me wonder what she was; a werewolf would have healed enough by now to not be limping. A werewolf would still have a hole in their ankle, but at least it wouldn't hurt as much now. Even Ruby, dimwitted, narcissistic Ruby would have been able to heal faster than Gigi could say ouch. As this thought raced through my head, just like so many other thoughts, Gigi tripped over a branch. Before she went face first into the ground, I caught her arm causing her to flinch although I had just saved her nose.

"I'm really sorry for attacking you," I said, putting as much innocence into my voice as I could.

"I knew you would. I was expecting it," she said straightening up. I let go of her arm with an astonished look on my face.

"What? How?" At this point I couldn't tell if I was more astonished or amazed—or maybe even angry. *Why can't people just tell me the truth?* I asked.

"Let me guess, you haven't figured it out yet, have you?" she asked, almost sympathetically as if she didn't think I would ever realize what was going on.

"Figure out what?" I asked, hopelessly, crossing my arms across my chest angrily.

I felt like a child once again. I felt like I used to before my mom died. She used to read me the best books ever. They always contained the right amount of suspense, action, mystery. But now I had to read them alone and imagine her soft voice, purring the text from the books. Her voice had always seemed so soothing. There was something about how she would read that made it seem as if she had written them herself.

Until just recently, she would always read me a story before I would go to bed. After that, there was always just something so comforting about being read a story to when you couldn't sleep. I had always thought it was more calming then a lullaby could ever be. Now tears were burning in my eyes. When would this misery end? I hated missing my mother so much and having a huge hole in my heart.

"I heard you guys talking at lunch on the first day of school," she said, causing my mind to go blank. This wasn't good. If she were to report us, the punishment could be death. "If you don't think I'm a werewolf, what do you think I am?" she asked, sounding curious rather then angry. For a second, I thought she was just going to spill and tell me everything. In the background, I could see the school slowly creeping up on us.

"You're not a mutant deer are you?" I asked, blurting out the first thing that came to my mind. Why a mutant deer came to mind, I wasn't entirely sure.

"No," she laughed. "Anyways, you'll find out soon enough," she finished as she started to limp off into the school, but then turned back to me to say one last thing. "Oh, and do me a favor and pay attention in school today.

It'll do you some good." Then she was gone; lost in the endless school, while I was left behind paralyzed in a confused state of shock. What was she talking about? Was I the only one who thought she was quite possibly crazy?

By now, Gigi was in the school. In the corner of my eye, I could see the blob standing a few feet behind me. It was odd. I couldn't remember it following us, but it was there. Also, what I thought was a horn at one point in time, was really a pony tail. I didn't know how I couldn't have noticed that, but somehow I managed to confuse the two. I turned around, quick as I could hoping to see more of it only to find myself staring off into space looking dumbfounded. It was just gone.

As I looked all around me, still hoping to see more, I noticed Ruby huddling around a tree; she was late just like me. She seemed to be having trouble walking through the bushes so I went over to help her. Of course Idiot Red never thought about walking around the bushes. Just like Gigi, she flinched at the sight of me.

"I'm fine," she said. She had an odd look on her face. The kind of look you would give someone if they had hit you upside the head or something. "Now…go away!" she yelled, shooing me away.

Suddenly I had the strangest Déjà vu feeling. Not to my surprise, Ruby tripped over a branch. Just as before with Gigi, I caught her arm before she completely busted her nose. I let go as soon as she had her feet properly on the ground again. "Um...thanks," she said making me wonder if that was the first time I had ever heard Ruby say 'thanks.'

It was funny the way she said it too. Like she was thinking more of what would have happened to her face then actually thinking about that fact that I actually saved her face so to speak. Then she straightened up. I just gave her a nod back. She seemed to be walking fine today, even after the attack. The claw marks on her face were barely visible, but they were there. They almost gave her a more daredevil look. I personally thought she looked way better like this then she did before. Something inside me thought that she would say differently however.

We walked into the school in an awkward silence. As we made our way to the classroom, we still didn't talk. As we walked into the classroom, everyone looked up awkwardly at us. Apparently we were walking 'together.'

It was odd because I didn't have any other clothes, currently, so I had to wear my torn up ones. There was a huge hole under my ribcage exposing the tear drop that Blair had carved into my skin in my dream. Though it hurt and wouldn't stop bleeding, I felt like it looked kind of awesome, almost like a tattoo.

Gigi was sitting in a chair at the front of the room; her foot was still raw, but it had somehow managed to stop bleeding where my claws had dug in with hopeless, self-centered rage.

I really didn't understand myself. There had been no reason to attack her. She didn't threaten me, or harm me in any way. Yet I still attacked her. And somehow she managed to forgive me.

"Zaina," Gigi said, sounding slightly awkward. "Ruby," she said as if she was giving her a warning through her vocal cords. "Sit," she finished, gesturing the two seats in front of her. Ruby decided to sit as close to Blaze as she could. As she did so, he looked over at Cy, and she nodded. They quickly switched seats and Ruby gave Cy a hateful look. Then she looked over at me.

"Switch seats with me, will ya?" she asked, as if sitting by Cy was a hellish nightmare she didn't wish to continue.

"Sure," I said, switching seats at last and smiling over to Cy. It was always nice to sit next to a close friend in class and communicate with facial expressions. Eventually, Ms. Gigi began class.

"Okay, we need to talk," she said, firmly, letting us know she meant business. However, she seemed to be faking concern. "As you all know, Ruby was attacked yesterday," she paused. "We aren't sure who did it," she paused once more, confirming that she was faking, "but we have been instructed to ask you all some questions."

"Are you going to ask me?" Ruby asked, as if she were the only princess allowed in this world.

"Yes," Gigi said simply as if the question in itself seemed unthinkable.

"Why? I mean I get that you're trying to figure out who attacked me and all, but I don't see why you would have to ask me. Why would I hurt myself? I mean seriously," she finished with an attitude. She couldn't grasp the concept that the pack leaders were trying to find out who attacked her.

"Just answer the questions!" I yelled. Everyone, but Gigi of course, looked at me in surprise.

"Geez, what's her probl—" I heard Bow say from behind me. Although he didn't get a chance to finish, I knew exactly what he was going to say. Then I heard an "Ow!" Only later did I realize that Cy had hit him upside the head.

After Ms. Gigi went over what we should write down, she passed out the thing she called 'paper.' It didn't feel like our usual paper and on top of that, it was as boring as a rock. Well come to think of it, a rock is sort of interesting with all its chips and cracks. They always told a story about where they'd been; what they'd been through. This paper was just… flat. And for some reason it felt soft unlike our usual rough paper.

"Okay then. Now that we all have paper, why don't we talk about what we're going to do once you're done," she said, beginning to go off on a tangent about humans.

As she talked, Cy came back from the bathroom. I had always thought it was odd how girls would only go to the bathroom to stare in the mirror and tell their usually beautiful selves that they looked hideous.

Cy passed my chair and gave me the look. Then she softly said, "We need to talk." Her voice was urgent yet cautious. She also didn't say it in the hostile way Ruby had the other day—it was more of a gentle tone in comparison.

For a second, I thought she was just going to tell me, because of the slight bit of frustration that was just barely detectable in her voice. As she walked back over to her seat, I caught a glimpse of Phantom giving Cy a warning glance. That's when I knew that the part about them talking yesterday at the field wasn't a dream.

As I continued to zone out, remembering more and more of the dream—all stuff I didn't want to remember— Gigi was talking. I was caught in a wild daze full of confusion, when Duke's bloody corpse flashed in front of my mind again. His voice echoed inside my head, "You did this to me…You did this to all of us. I wouldn't tell you… ever. I'm sorry." I gagged once more, remembering the awful smell of rotting flesh and bone.

I couldn't remember ever having a dream with smell to it. I also couldn't remember having a dream where it would change as I did things. A number of questions popped into my mind as it started racing again. The one question that stood out the most, though, was what did I do to all of them? Something else that stood out was—was I possibly seeing the future? At that moment I was worried that I was. *Will someone just kill me now?* I thought grimly.

"Zaina? Are you all right?" I heard Gigi ask as I came back to reality, only to zone out once more after seeing the blob—whatever it might be.

Then again, I saw Duke's corpse jump in front of me. He repeated the same line again, only this time they were all saying, no screaming, "You did this to me! You did this to all of us!"

Then they all became quiet. The last one to speak was Cy.

"I wouldn't tell you…ever. I'm sorry." There was more sorrow in her voice then there was in Duke's. Instead of hatred, there was sorrow. And instead of liveliness, there was distance. When I stopped zoning out I noticed Gigi was waving her hand in front of my face, too close for comfort.

"Hum?" I asked; for some reason, my confusion seemed amusing to everyone but Cy.

"Zaina, are you sure you're okay?" Gigi asked. I somehow knew she was expecting this kind of…behavior if that's what you want to call it. But looking into her eyes, you could almost tell she was more concerned then she thought she would be. Even she knew that I wasn't supposed to be acting like that.

"Yeah, I'm fine." I said. I suddenly became oddly happy. How does one go from being nonsocial to out-of-the-ordinary chipper in a split second?

"Okay…" Gigi almost seemed to roll her eyes in confusion. "So, on the piece of paper, you will be writing everything you did yesterday afternoon until this morning. Including dreams." For some odd reason, I got the feeling that she was directing the last part to me.

"What do dreams have to do with attacking Ruby?" Bow asked idiotically.

"Well when someone has done something wrong, they often feel guilt and these guilt's are sometimes portrayed in our dreams," she explained, with a smile.

"Okay then," I said, rolling my eyes. I wasn't too keen on exposing myself the way dreams usually did.

"So, you all know what to do I assume?" she said, looking out at all of us. Something inside me told me she knew we all just wanted her to stop talking and let us work.

"Yup!" Blaze said sarcastically. Only later did I realize he was being serious, which was highly unusual for someone who was never really serious.

Everyone started filling out the paper word by word. Our pencils wrote awkwardly on the soft paper. As you wrote, it made the most god awful noise that sounded like nails down a chalkboard. All the screeching was giving us headaches that felt like they would give us brain damage.

I had started to write when Gigi said, "Zaina, can I talk to you out in the hallway for a second?" She looked at me with pleading eyes, as if something was terribly wrong, but she didn't really care.

"No, I think I'll stay in here." I said, with my normal attitude before this year had begun. Now I was feeling rather cocky. She gave me another annoyed look. "I was just kidding. Gosh. And anyways, I don't have a choice, do I?" She shook her head indicating that I really didn't have a choice.

As usual, as I walked to the door, everyone—led by Ruby and Bow—decided to say ridiculous things such as "Oh, girl, you're in trouble." Typically, as Gigi and I left, they all began to talk.

Gigi looked at me and quickly said, "I need you to lie," her eyes pleading.

"What? No! What are you—crazy?" I said, feeling bewildered. I looked around feverishly to make sure no one was around. Though I'd attacked her, I didn't want to be blamed for it if everyone saw someone else do the deed.

"Please Zaina. It's safer this way," she explained, hoping I would understand. I hesitated for a moment but soon nodded. However, I was not at all happy with this situation.

"Okay," I began, as she pushed me towards the door. "But what should I say?" I asked, worriedly. I'd always been a horrible liar.

"I don't know—just make something up," she said, still pushing me. Before she could force me through the door, I stopped and looked at her.

"Remind me one more time why I'm doing this?" I asked, feeling rather irritated. If they found out I was lying, the punishment—as always—could be death. However, she simply looked at me frantically.

"I'll explain everything to you later," she said, her eyes wide with stress. "Now go inside and do your work!" she yelled, her tone harsh. I looked at her for a moment, confused about what had just happened. Then I saw an unknown teacher walking down the hall. *Smooth*, I thought, *what a good way to cover up the fact that you want me to lie and risk my own life.*

As we both walked back into the classroom, I thought about how amusing it was to see everyone scramble back to their desks and pretend they'd been working the entire time. Gigi simply sat behind her desk, pretending not to notice that everyone had gotten sidetracked.

"So how is everything coming along?" Gigi asked, grinning a dumbfounded grin and pretending she didn't care they weren't doing what they were supposed to be doing. As a few people spoke about the paper and how odd it was, I walked over and sat down at my desk.

Eventually, everyone settled back down for the most part. Phantom and Blaze, however, decided to throw paper balls back and forth. My nerves were beginning to run low as I sat staring aimlessly down at my paper, trying to come up with something. I was usually good at coming up with lies as long as I didn't have to tell it face-to-face, but not this time. The only word on my paper was 'sorry.' *That's odd*, I thought, *I don't remember writing that.*

It had seemed like only a few minutes when Gigi said, "Oh gosh, it's already lunch time." She almost seemed relieved. I would have been too if I were a teacher.

"But I'm not finished," Phantom said, holding up his paper and making a face as if he were thinking really hard. *Even though we all know that's the one thing he finds harder to do than not talking,* I thought mockingly. "I haven't finished telling you about my dream from last night where I got chased by a bunch of dead werewolves who were trying to get me to eat a chipmunk for some reason." Then his gaze landed on me. "I think you were one of the dead zombie things too, Zaina," he said, grinning his annoying, wicked grin.

"Aw, dreaming about me now are you? How touching." I said, jokingly, though he seemed to find that anything but funny.

"Trust me. I'd never do that," he said, sounding disgusted. *What is that supposed to mean?* I thought, wondering if I was repulsive.

"We'll finish them later!" Gigi said so suddenly she even scared Blaze—the guy who never got scared and could keep a straight face through literally anything. "We're going to be late for lunch. Now get moving," she said, sounding almost like a dictator.

Seeing how she was acting made me feel odd knowing how people felt around me while I was having the mood swings. Something inside me felt really bad for all the people who had to put up with me, and at the same time I felt really grateful that they were still here.

We got up in an awkward silence – suddenly afraid of our own usually happy and cheerful Ms. Gigi. We walked hastily to the door, wondering two things. 1. Why she had reacted that way, and 2. What was going to happen now?

As we walked down the hallway, still not saying a word, Gigi stalked after us. About half way there, she began to rub her head, warily. Something that really struck me as odd was that the second Gigi snapped it felt like a sudden relief came over me. It almost felt like a giant rock had been strapped to my back, and then it just... fell off. Like they say it feels like when a spell is lifted.

We finally got to the cafeteria, still not talking. *Gigi's probably enjoying the quiet,* I thought as we walked in. We walked over to our table and began to loosen up a bit, while Gigi still seemed a bit antsy. *She'll be okay,* I thought as we ran over to the lunch line.

It wasn't until I looked at the clock that I actually realized how late we really were. *All because Phantom couldn't shut up,* I thought, almost angrily. As usual I got my thick, juicy, raw steak. I, just like every other werewolf out there, loved the way blood gushed out the sides when I bit into it.

Once we were sitting in our neat, orderly set of seats they called a table, we talked. As usual, Bow started the conversation. "Geez Zaina. What happened to you?" He asked, staring down at my torn clothes and tear symbol that was still bleeding, as I bit into my steak.

"I don't know," I said in between gulps. He looked at me in bewilderment. "What? I can't remember." I finished, my voice rising a bit.

I looked over and noticed Cy devouring her steak too, when she said, "I know what happened." Phantom looked at her. She reached over and kicked him, making him wince a little in pain. Some part of me made me wonder if they would make a cute couple. "Byrd told me," she finished, simply, taking another bite of her steak.

I noticed her look over her shoulder as the door opened and an oddly familiar boy walked in. It wasn't until he got closer that I realized it was Duke. What on earth was he doing here? Did he know that the inside of this cafeteria could be the last thing he would ever see? All these worries rushed through my mind like the blood pumping faster and faster through my veins.

Some of the teachers who were part-time babysitters for us wolves and part-time security ran over to talk to Duke. They looked like they were ready to throw punches because their hands were clenched up into fists. However, before things got out of hand, Duke simply held out a note.

As the teachers read it, they began to back off. "Sorry." I heard a teacher—who's name I didn't know and still don't know even though I had him one year—say. All though I didn't remember that teacher, I could tell he didn't mean his apology. Duke hurriedly walked over to our table. I found it odd that he didn't even have to look for it—it was like he already knew where it was.

"Hey," he said, pushing Phantom out of his seat so he could sit next to me. "Have any of you seen Giz by any chance?" His expression was worried. The few of us at the table who knew Gizmo shook our heads to signal that we indeed hadn't seen him. All the while, Ruby had her eyes glued to him. When he noticed, he said, "Will you stop staring? It's creeping me out." Just then, I noticed she was staring at his fangs.

"Not as creepy as those fangs of yours," Cy said, taking another enormous bite out of her steak.

"So, you said you knew what happened," I said, directing my attentions to Cy. "Spill," I finished plainly, and though I was talking to Cy, Duke didn't seem to realize, or possibly care, that we'd been having a conversation prior to his arrival.

"I never said such a thing," he said, as I simply couldn't help gawk at him. Whenever I tried to be serious and discover the truth, there was always someone to make a joke of it.

"I was talking to Cy," I said, feeling rather irritated. Then I noticed I couldn't help stare at him. At first it was because he was being ridiculous, but in the end I found myself describing his features in my head. I looked over at Cy and the same thing happened. Soon, I found it impossible not to describe everything I looked at. I looked back over at Duke.

"Great, now I have two girls staring at me," he said, sounding slightly freaked out. I suddenly began thinking up an excuse.

"I'm trying to read your mind—so maybe someone will tell me what happened yesterday," I yelled slightly, Duke looking unconvinced.

"Well, if you would just have asked, I would have told you. No need to crack down on your supposed 'voodoo' magic! We are friends after all," he said laughingly, looking around at the food we were eating in disgust.

Ruby looked at me and said, "I need to hang out with you more." I just chuckled quietly to myself, knowing that would never happen.

"Then tell me," I said, dismissing Ruby's comment. I was eager—very eager. After all, I had no clue how much of last night's dream was really a dream. I didn't know when it started and on top of that, I wanted to know how I could possibly have hurt myself in a dream, unless it really happened.

"Well, first we were all at the butterfly scene out near Phantom's cave and then you decided you were going to run home to try and find your dad," he paused. "Then my sweet, nice, caring sis," he said with much sarcasm, "found you and you passed out. She said it was from shock or something. Then Byrd said something about you starting to get cut up and hurt and stuff for no real reason. And there was more, but I don't really feel like saying that right now," he said, his grin almost menacing.

"So, how did she get hurt?" Bow asked, as if he thought this was all just some play, or a story from one of the books he'd read.

"How are we supposed to know that?" Phantom snapped, almost seeming angry that we were talking about this subject with other people around.

"What part is it you don't want to tell me?" I asked Duke. There were so many questions being asked at that moment that were not being answered that I was beginning to become even more frustrated then I already was.

"Sorry, forgot," he said, shrugging. I could tell he was lying. *Just another thing to add to the book,* I thought warily.

Chapter 13

We ate the rest of our lunch talking about normal things like homework and gossip, because that's pretty much the only thing there was to talk about on a little island like this. Duke seemed hungry the whole time, yet he never ate. For a while, I almost seemed to have forgotten Duke wasn't one of us. He managed to fit in so well and he also seemed to be able to make the best out of everything, in any situation.

"How long are you staying?" Cy asked, curiously. For a moment, I thought Cy accepted Duke as a member of our little 'posse' as Ruby called it, but there was still some kind of fear in her eyes. And I didn't think it was about the chipmunk thing in the woods that day.

"Well, if Gigi doesn't mind I might as well stay the rest of the day," he said, smiling and flashing his pearl white teeth. *I don't remember us mentioning her name,* I thought.

"Great, just another annoying person to add the class," I said jokingly, though with my luck he would most likely take it literally.

"I feel the love, I really do," he said, putting his hand over his heart. While some would snap back an ignorant, usually lame come back at me, Duke always decided to play along. I just chuckled back, taking the last bite of my steak and savoring it—almost as if there were none left in the world and this was the last time I was going to eat.

Suddenly, Ms. Gigi called for us to leave. We all hesitated for a moment, but I decided to be the brave one and got up first. Next to follow was Duke. I was almost certain that he would have been the one to get up first, but he didn't. It was weird—it wasn't like he knew her or anything. Or did he?

"It's about time," she said, causing me to wonder. Just like I had been, Gigi seemed abnormally cheerful. Now for some reason, I had that same feeling of anger in the pit of my stomach that I had before I came to school today. How was it that we seemed to be trading emotions?

"Why so chipper?" Blaze asked, after having caught up with us. As usual, Cyprus was trailing behind him.

"I feel better somehow," Gigi said, almost sounding like a dolphin; her voice rasping in my ears like nails down a chalkboard. I almost liked the moody Gigi better than the overly happy one.

We walked to our class room, this time scared of our teacher because she was dancing and humming strange tunes all the way there. Why was she acting so suddenly different?

When we were finally in the classroom, we were instructed to finish our papers. While I was mustering up some kind of convincing lie, everyone else was hopefully telling the truth. Eventually I managed to come up with something like this:

I left school

Went into the woods with Ruby and Duke

Ruby got attacked

I paused for a minute—remembering something Blair had said. *You were trying to help her!* Then I continued.

Helped fight off the thing that attacked Ruby

Went to go and see the butterflies with the boxes

Talked to a few people

Ran home

Went to sleep

Then I was suddenly stumped. I was wondering if I should have said I didn't have the dream and if I should have I mention I passed out. I could only imagine that causing the pack leaders to worry.

Dreamt about magical pixie ponies

Went to school with Gigi

Was at school

I really wanted to put the word "duh" after the last bullet, but in the end decided against it. I figured it would get me in trouble—if I wasn't already in trouble.

After mustering up something that was somewhat, yet at the same time entirely not true, I turned my paper in. Then came the time when Gigi had instructed me to pay attention. The fact that she had to tell me made me wonder if she thought I even paid attention at all.

Though some people found it rather irritating, I found it rather entertaining how Ms. Gigi was suddenly so giddy she couldn't stop laughing. As she stood at the front of the room trying to be serious, she said, "Okay," she tried to say, bursting into laugher once more. "Now we're going to learn about," she began, though suddenly looked around the room and settled her eyes on me.

Then she walked up, and passed me. That was when I realized she had been looking at Phantom, who was currently sitting directly behind me, slouched over in his seat, asleep and almost drooling. "Humans!" she yelled in his ear.

Phantom jumped straight up in his seat and yelled,

"Where? Don't tell them!" Gigi exploded into another fit of hysterical laughter as if she were drunk.

"Nowhere; you were sleeping, genius." I said annoyed, crossing my arms across my chest.

At first, I hadn't even thought about what he'd said. I just thought it was some strange 'Phantom thing.' However, when I started thinking about it, it sort of made sense. When he said 'where' he might have been talking about the humans. And then he said, 'don't tell them.' Could it be possible that humans were still, somehow, alive somewhere?

"So, on to our lesson," she said, glancing at me as if to remind me that I should pay attention; I found unexplainably irritating.

I'm not Phantom, people! I actually pay attention, I thought, *and I don't drool in my sleep*, I finished, thinking about the last time he was asleep with his head on his desk. Once he lifted his head, a glaze of not-so-pleasant drool was visible on the desk. "Well the humans are," Gigi began, stopping herself, "I mean were very social. Like we do, they lived with their parents for the first half of our life," she finished, weaving her fingers together in front of her.

Duke interrupted and said, "Um, excuse me? I'm the same age as everyone else in this room, except you of course, and I don't live with my parents." He had a sly smirk on his face that made him look like a dare deviling misfit.

I cut in and said, "Yeah and my mom died and my dad split, so where does that put me?" I had somewhat of the same look on my face, though making a joke out of my mother's death hit me hard for a moment; I somehow managed to disregard the fact that she was gone, making me feel even worse for practically forgetting her. She gave us both a look that said, clear as day, 'keep it up and I'll keep singing,' causing both of us to shut up.

"I'm talking about the average werewolf your age," Gigi snapped stubbornly and sounding mildly annoyed.

Blaze opened his mouth as if he wanted to add something but Gigi cut him off as quickly as she could. "Let's continue," she said as if this was the last thing in the world that we could do.

As she said this, Blaze mimicked her; she simply rolled her eyes at him. Sometimes she seemed to act more like a child then an adult in her 20's. Something inside me told me that she was too young to be a teacher.

"They lived in differently sized things called houses. This is where they mostly ate, slept, and even hung out with their friends and family, like we do. As you will read in the diaries—which you will either be getting tomorrow or the day after—they had to go to school, too. They learned very different things, though," she said, pausing and looked around the room as if anticipating a sleeping student.

"They learned about history, like we are doing right now, only a different type of history of course. They also learned about their government, which was run by somebody called the president and a few other branches of government. They learned different types of science, which was about nature, the universe and how we're made. Another really cool thing they learned was math," she said, turning around to draw a number of odd symbols on the board.

Suddenly Bow yawned unnecessarily loud and said, "When are we going to learn about what happened to them?" For the first time in history, we actually agreed on something.

"Oh I'm sorry, am I boring you?" she said, looking at us oddly. We all nodded, hoping we could skip ahead in our curriculum. "Well get over it. You have to know this stuff," she said, sounding almost like a teenager; this was an example of one of her 'immature moments.'

As the day went on, she continued to lecture us on different aspects of human life. However, the day seemed to be never ending. When the bell finally rang, she said, "Oh well, see you guys tomorrow," with a friendly wave. "You can look forward to learning how the humans…died," she said, once again having trouble talking about the strange humans' extinction. However, something inside me was now determined to think that Gigi, herself, was a human.

Chapter 14

I began to head towards my cave, after having collected all I needed from the school for the night. Ever since they'd found out about my parents, they decided they were going to provide me with a breakfast, lunch, and dinner for free. I, personally, was offended by that. Werewolves were always known for having fragile egos, and treating them as if they were two years old and unable to hunt for themselves was not a way to go about business.

As I started to walk into the woods, I remembered that Gigi had said she wanted to talk. I turned around, thinking. It was odd, not having Duke around. Sometimes, he felt like a shadow. Thinking of this also made me wonder what it must be like for him, Byrd and Giz to read minds.

Was it hard to hack into someone's brain? Did they often get headaches from it? All these questions would probably remain unanswered—at least for now. Not only did I wonder about those strange aspects of the butterflies, but I also thought about how different I was compared to the beginning of that school year.

I had seemed so innocent then; everything had seemed

so simple. I didn't have to constantly hope no one made me mad, because of my unconventional temper tantrums I'd been having. I also didn't think about everything I was told, because it didn't matter then. Now I was expected to save the world—apparently for the second time.

As I walked back to the school, a younger girl and her friend blurred by me; skipping and laughing. *I was that happy once,* I thought, sadly. I then felt a sudden chill go down my back and into the ground. I looked around, wondering why this chill suddenly fell upon me. Suddenly, I noticed the blob just to my right. However, just as I saw it, it vanished.

As it disappeared, another girl walked by. She was alone. She looked sad and lonely, like I was sure I did—and felt for that matter. Looking all around me, I then noticed just how beautiful my surroundings truly were.

The trees, with their elegance—swaying back and forth to the soft, sweet sound of the crackling wind. The flowers spoke for themselves. If they had a voice, I would imagine them singing a sad, sweet melody that reminded me of running water. They would sing with the chirping crickets that hid in the tall grass. Then there was the grass itself. If grass could somehow magically transform into a person, I would imagine it to be someone with great courage, who never stops moving and never gives up. This was something I was hoping, and was expected to be.

Suddenly, I saw a hand wave to me, coming from inside the school. Gigi walked out; Cy, Blaze, Duke, and Phantom all trailing obediently behind her. They all had the same look on their faces. Like they were instructed to remain silent, or else they would get in serious trouble.

As they walked up to me, Gigi was the only one to talk. "Zaina, I'm so glad you remembered," she said, once again using a dolphin voice too high-pitched and shrill for my tired ears.

"Oh, yeah. I sure am, too," I said sarcastically, wondering if she could tell I was bluffing.

"Okay. Follow me. I need to go to my house and then I'll tell you everything you need to know," she said, suddenly become serious. I was suddenly beginning to become angry again, and something told me she could tell. As I got even more mad, Gigi started to lose the little bit of color she had in her face. As they normally did when I was mad, my claws grew.

Then I said, as calmly as I could, "Why don't you tell me here?" There was an odd edge to my voice as I tilted my head to the side.

She began to stutter. "Um, I can start telling you," she paused, as if to think, "along the way," she finished, hurriedly. Although she was trying to act calm, I could still tell by the look in her eyes that she was scared.

"Then let's start walking," I said, turning away from them—not actually caring to look back to see if they were following me or not. Something told me that they would catch up even if they didn't want to. And even though I had no clue where to go, I kept walking, keeping a steady pace.

By now, I had calmed down. Gigi was walking beside me, basically explaining the same things she had in class. Cy, Blaze, Duke, and Phantom were still trailing behind in an awkward silence.

I thought it was rather odd that Cy wasn't babbling about humans. In some strange way, I almost wished she would. Ever since Gigi's mood swings, she had been talking with an odd cautious, unawareness that almost seemed to scare me. She was always such a lively person, that I thought would never die—even in the afterlife I can imagine her being cheerful. But now all that was left was a shell. Like something had happened to her. Almost like she had forgotten something. For a while, I even wondered if she knew who she was.

We got to a narrow road that forked out to two roads, not three. As we went down the left, Cy went down the right. "Hey Cy? Aren't you coming with us?" I yelled. It seemed like our lives were flashing before our eyes, that was how long it took for her to react. Then she finally said, "I-I'm go going h-home. See you to tomorrow." Out of all the things Cy was well known for, stuttering wasn't one of them. Again, all the liveliness seemed to be drained. Now all that was left was a lifeless, black hole. There was neither humanity nor wolf left in her. She was just a shell. Even Gigi was shocked.

"Um, Cy? Your house is in the other direction," Blaze finally said after we all stared at each other in confusion.

"I… oh…," she said, seeming so lost and confused. "I knew that." She turned around and started to walk again, still in the wrong direction. Blaze looked worried.

"I think I'm gonna go with Cy," he said. I gave him a sympathetic nod, trying to cover up my smirk; we all knew his worries were coupled with affection.

"You do that." I said, thinking about when the day would come when they finally admitted they were perfect for each other. Eventually, we continued walking; Gigi still repeating what she had said in class.

After a while, we had come up to a smallish, rectangular shaped box thing. It obviously didn't look like a cave, and it didn't really look too much like the houses Cy and Gigi had shown us. However, it was missing the normal shape and the clique white picket fence we had always seen in pictures at school. I was surprised I'd never seen it before! It was huge compared to a cave.

On the inside, it felt cluttered and cramped. I had a strange feeling of claustrophobia. Though the outside was an odd drab color, the inside had dark purple walls with navy curtains. The inside reminded me of a midnight sky after a harsh and extreme thunderstorm. In comparison to the outside, I definitely liked the inside much more then I did the outside.

As I walked into what I thought at first was a black hole, I saw the blob walk in with us. I wonder if Gigi knew what it was. If only she or whoever knew would tell me. Whenever I saw it, I almost felt desperate—as if something inside me knew the blob, but just couldn't remember it. So far, the only thing I'd recognized was a ponytail.

"Please, sit down." Gigi said, pointing to a boxy looking thingamabob sitting in the corner.

I suddenly realized I had been day dreaming until now. For some reason, her pendants caught my eyes. However, there was one that seemed to catch my eye the most as the sun's rays glinted on its gold chain. It was the shape of a tear drop and the color of the strange sweet substance humans that we learned humans ate, called honey. As it winked at me, I robotically walked over to it, somehow strangely hypnotized. Not only did it wink but it almost felt like it was calling my name—as if it wanted me to have it.

"That would be the pendant of control," Gigi said, following my obvious gaze. I must have looked like a kid in a candy shop, even though this time nothing was edible. "Something you could probably use right now," she finished, taking the gold necklace off the rack, separating it from its brothers and sisters. As she set it around my neck, the odd calling finally stopped.

As it lay around my neck, I indeed felt like I could control anything. The teardrop itself had looked bigger on the rack alongside all the others. On me, it felt perfect. Whether it was the size or the supposed purpose of the pendant, I wasn't quite sure. All I knew was that when I wasn't wearing it, it badgered me until I put it on again; almost like it was lonely.

Looking down on it, I noticed it was the same tear Blair had carved just under my ribcage in my dream. I still couldn't believe I'd actually gotten hurt even though it was just a dream.

"It's called a soul necklace. All werewolves, butterflies, and the occasional human will get one if they play a major role in a prophecy. Witches will even get one if they prove themselves worthy enough," Gigi said, glancing at her other pendants, passing her index finger through them. There was one with a target and an arrow, a dead, bleeding rose, a heart that had been stabbed with blood dripping out the side of it, a running rabbit, what looked like a compass, and an almost transparent mask.

The bleeding rose looked oddly familiar. Not only was it odd, but it was beautiful in a way only the deceased could understand. The rose itself looked kind of dead with its black petals. On the left side, blood was dripping—no gushing out. Whoever it belonged to must have been charming—hence the rose—but at the same time, really strong and able to do a lot of damage—hence the blood. As I thought this, I suddenly thought about how much that sounded like Duke.

As I gazed at the other pendants that I couldn't really relate to anyone else I knew, I thought again about my pendant and how the same image was carved into my skin. I wondered if it would heal over, or if it would remain a tear shaped scar.

"So, what's the point of these again?" I asked, indicating the other pendants including mine.

"Well yours, for example, is supposed to help you control yourself. See, your problem is that you are basically too strong for your own good, and the animal inside you is trying to take over. But with that necklace, you will have all your strength, but at the same time you'll be able to control yourself along with that temper of yours," she answered.

That wasn't necessarily what I wanted to hear, but it was still an answer.

"So, basically without this I'd go all psycho-wolf?" I asked, raising an eyebrow, glancing down at my necklace once more.

"Yeah, sure. Some even said you would go crazy enough to destroy yourself as well as many others," she said, though she sounded skeptical.

"Oh, that sucks. For you guys' sake, I'll wear this 24/7. I can't imagine 'crazy Zaina' being a beautiful sight," I said, sarcastically. While Duke chuckled a tad, Gigi just gave me a quick look that said anything but 'ha-ha.' "So," I changed subject, "you said you were going to tell me how the humans died." Before, I would have definitely sounded pushy. I guess the pendant was working more than I had expected it to.

"Oh, yeah…that," she said with a sad look on her face again as she walked over to the boxy thing in the corner and sat down on it.

"Are you by any chance human?" I asked uncertainly.

"A human?" she asked, chuckling lightly. "No, no, no.

I'm a witch though." *She's not a human?* I thought, disappointedly. I thought I had things straight by now.

"Then why do you always get such a depressed look on your face whenever someone mentions the 'h' word?" I asked, seeming rather pushy.

"Because," she began, rubbing her temples. "I witnessed it all. The tornado, the mutation, and then the flood. It's a very horrible sight… seeing all your friends and family mutating and going crazy… *killing* everything in sight," she said, sounding horrified. "See what happened was, one day they were calling for tornados. While the tornados made their way to some of the smaller populations, they crossed paths with some nuclear reactors.

'A nuclear reactor is basically a big box that used nuclear energy and transformed it into electricity for humans. However, they needed to be cooled by water. As these tornados came, they broke the reactor's water and they exploded.

'Although the good news is that not every single reactor was hit. That's how the 'wolf syndrome', as some called it, was created. Somehow the radioactive waves made people go crazy and act like wolves. Over time, they just became wolves somehow. Still to this day, there are questions to be answered.

In the end, everything that wasn't destroyed by the tornados was destroyed by the people who got infected. This next part might sound a little crazy, but they actually had some of the few remaining dog trainers come and help the people who got infected control themselves. It was the only way," she said, looking as if she was about to burst into tears.

"So, I have two questions. How did *you* not get infected? And wouldn't the mutation spread since it's technically a virus?"

"Well, somehow witches are immune to the waves. Even some humans were immune," she explained. "There was one witch named Adamè who managed to create a spell that stopped the virus from spreading over the entire earth just in time," she paused, as if waiting for another question.

"So, I'm confused. How did the butterflies come into the picture?" I asked, glancing at Duke for a moment.

"Some people, somehow, were affected differently by the virus. We don't really know why or where the blood thirst and wings came from. All we know is that some people were immune, along with the witches; some became werewolves as they call them now, and some became giant carnivorous butterflies. If it weren't for Adamè, there would be no more people at all. And without people, there would be no food for werewolves and butterflies. Only the elder wolves know about the humans, however. This is considered highly classified because they don't want too many people knowing the truth. However, if they didn't help us at all, that would mean," she began, though I didn't bother to let her finish.

"Yeah, yeah I know. No more anything on earth. That's actually depressing." I interrupted, thinking about how much we suddenly relied on this supposed extinct species.

"It gets worse," she said, forebodingly. "A little while after the tornados and the mutation, there was a massive flood. No one really knows where the water came from. Christians thought it was merely a repeat of Noah's Ark. The Wiccans thought that Mother Earth was mad at us for polluting her. Then some scientists believed that the earth's axis somehow changed and the North Pole moved into a warmer climate and all the melted ice created the flood. Like

I said, no one really knows.

But when the water came, the witches, werewolves, humans, and butterflies all fled to higher ground. Some of the werewolves and butterflies were kind enough to transport the humans and witches. If it weren't for them, there would probably be none of us left. That's really the only reason the humans made a deal with the mutants, as they would call you," she said, making a face as if she didn't appreciate the term 'mutant.'

"Wait a second; today I thought about the possibility that maybe humans still existed," I said, though in the end it sounded a bit more like a question.

"Wow, you're smarter then you look," Gigi said, suddenly lightening up a bit as if she thought the world could be saved after all.

"I knew I wasn't stupid!" I exclaimed, happily. I wasn't quite sure why I was so excited.

"Yeah well, no one said you were smart either," Phantom joked, making me realize that he was in the room with us; I'd forgotten about him somehow.

"Thanks," I mumbled sarcastically, rolling my eyes.

"Do you remember that time you talked to Ellen?" Gigi asked as I nodded. "Well, she said she was from Hollings right?"

I nodded again but then exclaimed, "Wait a second—I *am* stupid! When she said she was from an island with more of a variety of creatures, she was talking about there being humans too!" It felt like my brain was churning faster than a butter maker.

"Yup," she said, closing her eyes as if her head was hurting. I walked up to Phantom and punched him as hard as I could without breaking bones.

"Ow! What was that for?" he yelled in astonishment.

"Why didn't you tell me?" I yelled in his face, feeling angry once more.

"I—I wasn't supposed to!" he said, giving Gigi an accusing look.

"That is true. Everyone was told not to tell you too much because you were supposed to find out on your own," she said, as if that justified something.

"Why? If you wanted me to save the world so badly then why didn't you just tell me about the humans and all this other crap in the first place?" I asked so plain it somehow angered Gigi. Her expression changed so suddenly it started making me nervous—even with the necklace.

"You think this is all just crap?" she asked, a spark on anger visible in her eyes as her expression darkened.

"Oh boy," Duke mumbled as if he were expecting this to happen.

"I never meant it like that," I said defensibly. It seemed that this time I wouldn't have anyone standing up for me because they all seemed to think she was right.

"This isn't crap!" her voice suddenly raised to a yell. "This is very important! Think about all the helpless children and adults that will die if you don't help them. You can't just neglect your sacred duty like this!" she practically yelled as she started walking closer and closer to me. I really hadn't expected her to get so angry.

"Okay, okay. Gosh, it's not crap! I can obviously see that you're so unhappy to the point where you have to take your anger out on me because you don't have anything better to do. I didn't do anything wrong, okay? And I'm sorry if my way of saying 'stuff' offends you!" I yelled as I turned to walk out the door. "Oh—and by the way, I do care. I never said I didn't," I finished, anger pumping through my veins like a disease.

Then I was gone; out of there. I wanted to cry out of uncontrollable frustration, but somehow the necklace wouldn't let me. I still had so many questions. What deal did they make? Who was Gigi talking about when she said 'they?' Why did she have anger issues? Oh, and then most important question. How was I supposed to save the world?

As I asked myself these questions, I heard the door fly open from behind me. Oh, how I wished it could be my mom or dad, coming to cheer me up somehow, but as it turns out it was—Phantom? Of all the people to send, he was the person I wanted to see the least.

"What do you want?" I said, insensitively. The look on his face was nearly priceless.

"Well that's harsh," he said, rolling his eyes. "I'm coming to talk to you about something." I looked at his as if he were crazy. He was just so…serious. I never thought I'd see him like this.

"Shoot," I said, looking through the window of Gigi's

house, seeing her give Duke the bleeding rose soul necklace. *Guess I was right,* I thought.

"I think you'll like this actually. Gigi told me that you needed to be trained with weapons, so she thought me and Byrd could do that," he said. *Hum, weapons? Sounds good,* I thought amusingly.

"Cool," I said simply, finding vague answers amusing all of a sudden.

"So, is that a yes?" he asked anxiously, slightly jumping up and down.

"Sure," I replied, once again as vaguely as I could. Phantom had no idea how amusing this was to me.

"Okay," he said, happily. "So when do you want to meet up to start training?" he asked, looking quite excited.

"I don't know," I said, shrugging as I started walking away.

"Okay, I'll tell Byrd to come get you like tomorrow or something," he yelled after me as I continued to walk.

"You do that," I mumbled just loud enough so he could scarcely hear me.

"What?" he yelled after me.

"I said, you do that!" I yelled banshee style. I hope I didn't hurt his feelings in some awkward way. Yet as much as I pretended I cared, I realized just how much I really didn't.

The Novus Proprius Chronicles

Chapter 15

I ran off not even bothering to see if Phantom had anything more to say. *As if he didn't already say enough*, I thought. As I walked home, to my surprise I thought about my hair. I still had a couple hours before dark came so I decided to go down to Miranda, the best and only hairdresser on the island.

Miranda wasn't her real name. No one knew what it really was. Really, all people know about her was that she did literally everyone's hair and that she was a very sweet 29 year old, that somehow had naturally forest green hair that was even curlier then Byrd's.

It took me about ten minutes to get down to her little shop called 'Awesome Waves.' It seemed like a relatively quiet night, so I figured I wouldn't have to wait too long. And I was right.

As it turns out, I was the only person in her shop at that one quiet moment when I entered. I was actually kind of scared of what my new hair style was going to look like. Up until now, I had always had my hair extremely long, almost down to my butt. Now—tired of always having to mess with it—I was planning on getting it cut all the way up to my shoulders.

"Hello?" I called, unable to see Miranda in the tiny shop. I heard a small groan coming from the bathroom. "Hello?" I yelled again, warily this time.

"Yes?" Miranda said so suddenly that I jumped—despite the power of the pendent. As she talked to me, she dried her hands. It almost looked like some kind of red fluid was staining them. Looking at it, I could tell that it was either blood or hair coloring. However, if there was someone with hair that color red, literally everyone would know about it by now. Word traveled fast on that island, which could be a bad thing sometimes.

"Oh dear, I'm sorry! I didn't mean to scare you like that!" she said, with her odd Puerto Rican accent.

"Oh you're fine, I just didn't know you were back there." I said, dismissing the red on her hands. For the first time in a long time, I gave someone other than my parents a smile that I actually meant, yet I didn't get one back. That seemed very unlike Miranda. She always had a smile—for everyone. Even lost souls could get a smile out of her.

"So what is it that you want today?" She said, taking a quick glance at the bathroom before looking back at me.

"Um, I was hoping you could cut it up to my shoulders," I said. As hard as she was trying to convince me she was paying attention, I could tell she really wasn't.

"Yeah, sure. You want layers with that?" she suggested.

I shrugged and said, "Sure," despite the fact that I have no clue what layers were. Then she set to work. This usually over talkative person wouldn't peep a word as she began to snip and snip.

As she continued to cut, I couldn't help but notice the crisp snip sound as she cut her scissors through my healthy, thick hair. As it hit the floor, I felt a jab of sorrow hit me. There was something about losing my hair, hearing the 'thud' sound as it hit the floor, the 'snip' that made me… sad. And then there was something else; something that I couldn't quite place my finger on.

At first I thought that sorrow was coming from me losing my hair, for some reason, but there was something else; something that I wasn't realizing. Something that was secret—and menacing. It was an odd feeling. Only later did I realize what that feeling was for.

As I sat there getting my hair cut, about to cry for reasons I couldn't fathom, I couldn't help but hear a sluggish, sleepy, almost injured sounding groan coming from the bathroom, again. After she had finished, I glanced quickly into the mirror even though my mind was elsewhere. I couldn't help but wonder if curiosity really did kill the cat. Testing that theory, I went into the bathroom aimlessly, not sure what to expect.

While most bathrooms around here had only one stall, this bathroom had two. As I walked in, I noticed that there was a stench in the air. Just like that feeling of sorrow I had felt earlier, I couldn't quite put my finger on what kind of smell it was.

I checked the first stall, my eyes not really looking, my nose going crazy, and my mind racing. I stared down at the floor—there was a puddle of blood. It looked as if it had been there for only a little while, yet at the same time it looked like it had been moved somehow; almost like it had been dragged. I bent over to look under the stall's wall. Surprisingly, the thought running wildly through my mind was, *I hope no one's in the other stall or else something really awkward is about to happen.*

Just like the one I was crouching in, this stall was forsaken, only there was a bigger puddle of blood. Yet at the same time, there seemed to be no signs of life in this stall. *Why does someone as sweet as Miranda have puddles of blood in her bathroom?* I thought, worriedly.

As I got back up, I noticed I had gotten some blood on my leg. Just great. Not only was my leg still bleeding through the bandages, now I also had some unknown person or animal's blood on my leg.

As I took some toilet paper and started rubbing the blood stain off, I heard another groan only this time it was right by my ear. It sounded like a mix between a bear growl and Ruby's scream, only quieter. I spun around as quick as I could, swinging my arms aimlessly hoping to hit something, only to be disappointed in the end. As I looked around, my nose blazing, I saw nothing. Only now the scent was stronger. Up close, it was the undeniable stench of the undead.

I stepped out of the stall and looked around. This undead thing seemed to be playing hide-and-go-seek because I couldn't see it, but I could smell it. I was about to leave when I felt a tap on my shoulder. As quick as a snap, I spun around and this time I did manage to hit something. As our arms collided, warm blood splattered everywhere.

It was running down my face now. Running down my cheek like tear drops, dripping down my forehead like sweat, and running off my arms like rain. I wasn't sure where all this blood was coming from or even how so much of it had gotten on me just from one hit. The blood burned; it even bubbled on my skin. But I didn't care. When I looked at the thing I noticed it was a girl.

Half her face was torn off, revealing a chipped up skull that looked like it had seen better days. The other half that was left was cut up, as if someone had stuck her through a shredder hopping to hurt her, but still keep her alive. The rest of her body had holes here and there—in her leg, her arms, and even her rib cage had a four inch hole in it. You could see right through her in some places.

She swung a limp arm at me. I didn't even hit her and her arm fell off. She simply picked it up and clipped it back in as if it were the most normal thing in the world, revealing more gushing blood and raw bone. As I looked closer to it, I noticed that her blood was more of a dark pink color. *Pink*?

I questioned myself. I never thought I would see pink blood. I'd hear about evil souls having black blood and truly good folks having blood that shimmered as if glitter had polluted it, but I had never heard of pink blood.

As I fought this zombie girl, she smirked a menacing grin at me. But as much as I convinced myself that this girl was evil, I had an odd feeling that she was somehow good. Though she was nearly invincible and dead, I had a gut feeling that I shouldn't be fighting her. She swung another limp, bloody arm at me, but instead of ripping her arm off— which was an idea—I hung on to it. She didn't pull back, to my surprise. I looked into her eyes, and saw something. Something that wasn't evil. In a way, she almost seemed lonely.

"What's your name?" I asked. This was probably pointless, but it was worth a try. The girl's mouth was moving, but no sound was coming out. *Poor girl*, I thought.

"Do you know why you're here?" I asked. The girl nodded, and again tried to say something. But as before, nothing came out.

This made me wonder once again why someone like

Miranda would bring someone like this girl back from the dead? It wasn't smart; it was pointless, cruel, and unnecessary. Though the girl knew why she was here, I hardly doubt it was for a good reason.

"Are you in pain?" I asked, and as she nodded again a wave of pity moved over me.

Then I saw her mouth the words, "Please kill me!" I let go of her hand and asked, "You sure?" She nodded once more, only she had an evil smirk again. This time, I wouldn't show her sympathy. Now the loneliness was replaced with evil and a thirst for blood. I had no choice but to kill her. It didn't work out as well as I would have hoped however.

First, her left arm flew into the sink with a loud 'thud.' Blood spewed out of her left shoulder blade, some hitting me in the face, the blood bubbling up like poison. She looked down at her arm, and went to go pick it up with her right arm, but then that one went tumbling down with the other one. This time blood spilt into my left eye, and as it bubbled up, I could have sworn I was going blind.

The pain felt like thousands of tiny needles piercing my eye. I rubbed my eye, and moved on. *If I could just get her head off, I think I'll be good,* I thought as I swung, my aim less accurate considering only one eye was fully functional.

She tried snapping at my arm like a rabid dog, but soon stopped as I heard a whistle coming from behind me. She straightened up, and just stood there. She had gone from rabid to docile because of one simple whistle.

I took advantage of the situation and knocked her head off. Her head was still emotionless as it lay on the ground. It was almost as if someone had taken away the little bit of life she had left in her. This time I was smart enough to remember to block the blood from getting on my face. One thing was for sure—I couldn't save the world blind. However, I was worried that I already was in one eye.

I turned around, hoping to find the person who had whistled only to see nothing. I took a quick glance at the mirror. *Layers are pretty cute, whatever they are,* I thought to myself. I did have to admit that it was kind of scary to see myself without long hair. I guess it would just have to be a while before I would get used to it. *Why am I worried about my hair and not this zombie beside me?* I thought, wondering where my humanity had gone.

I heard the zombie girl moan again. I looked down at her, just in time to see her vanish, leaving behind burgundy powder. The bubbles on my skin disappeared, but the stinging sensation in my eye was still there. Was this some kind of test that Gigi had set up for me to see how well I could fight? There were so many things about that woman that I thought I would never understand.

I walked out of the bathroom, and the first thing I noticed was that Miranda was gone, but another girl was there. *That's odd*, I thought. I didn't even know Miranda had an assistant, assuming that was who the blonde girl was. I started my way back to my lonely cave. *At least now I know who I'm fighting*, I thought to myself.

Chapter 16

I walked out of the hair salon and noticed just how dark it was. I had no idea that I had been in there for that long. If I wasn't going to kill Miranda for being evil, I was going to kill her for cutting off my natural scarf which I usually used to cover myself up when I was cold.

As I walked home, I noticed an uncertain chill in the air which made me feel as though something was going to happen—yet as far as I knew, nothing was supposed to happen.

Walking though the dense woods made me start to think a little extra about tonight. I couldn't help but remember how alike Miranda and the zombie girl had looked. They both had the tan skin and the high cheek bones. The only difference was the hair—Miranda had green hair and zombie girl had either blonde or pink hair—I couldn't quite tell from her blood dripping out of it. I knew this wasn't much to go on, but I thought they were somehow related.

What was I going to do? I finally had a lead on the person who I was supposed to stop, but something inside me told me that I shouldn't tell Gigi because I didn't think she would understand my suspicion. I looked down at my necklace. I noticed a drop of blood sizzled into the side of it. For some reason, I looked down at the pendent as if it was a child and I was its mother. The moon was shining through the tree branches like a spot light, and there was something both sweet and sinister about the look, yet I still couldn't help but want to baby it.

After having established that the blood was going to stay—partly because it couldn't come off and also because I thought it made it look cool—I continued my way through the endless forest back to my forsaken cave.

With both my mom and my dad gone, it looked suddenly huge. Before it was always cluttered with wolves, but now all that remained was a dead, soulless fire that looked like it hadn't been used in years.

There was a sudden urge, deep in the depths in my heart, to be held and to be told that I was loved. Usually my mom was the one that babied me. You could always tell if she loved you or not, by looking into her eyes. My dad was a different story, however.

He was like a locked door. You could never get him to open up to his feelings, and he never admitted anything either. On top of being a closed door, he was also like a giant bear in size. He was born with heavy shoulders, made to kill and pounce. My mom on the other hand—she was small and petite; designed to stalk and run. I guess I inherited both traits. The only thing I was missing was the skill and technique they had.

I noticed that while I was fighting the zombie girl, I let my guard down and I was just swinging my arms. There was no skill in that. I didn't even think as I swung. So maybe I would take those lessons with Byrd and Phantom. After all, who says no to weapons?

I went to bed without the pendant. I didn't even know why I took it off in the first place. Something just told me to—so I did. I fell asleep almost immediately, exhaustion washing over me. I had fallen asleep so suddenly, I didn't even notice that I had gone to bed hungry.

My dream was an odd toss of images.

I'm at school. I'm talking to Gigi, but she's wearing a mask. I don't know how I know it's her. I just know somehow. She pulls out a knife and starts chasing after me with it. I'm trying to run and scream, but no sound comes out and I can't move. As hard as I try to scream, only wisps of air escape and I can feel my lungs start to cave in as if I'm drowning. Gigi is about to stab me. Now I'm in a river that is about to go down a water fall. I'm trying to swim away, but I can't do anything. I feel that drowning feeling again, only this time, it feels more real. I begin to wonder if this is a dream at all.

As I fall to my near death, the scene changes. There is a girl and she's walking down the hallway, alone, her head bent down as if she's ashamed. She's wearing black skinny jeans, black converse, a black short sleeve top with a red tank top under it, black fishnet gloves up to her elbows and a red choker hangs around her small delicate neck.

People are yelling things at her like 'hey Emo girl! Need another razor?' and 'go hang yourself!' The girl just walks on. You can tell she's about to cry, and that what they say about her isn't true. But she doesn't do anything about it—she just walks on, all by herself.

The scene changes again. Now I'm at Miranda's hair salon. I'm in the bathroom. I see the scene where I was trying to talk to the zombie girl. This time, she talks back.

"What's your name?" I say.

"Diliah," the girl says. She has a beautiful voice.

"Do you know why you're here?" I ask, feeling more pity for her then ever.

"Yes, to stop you." Now her voice turns grim, and I can see the good in her eyes fading away.

"Are you in pain?" I ask, almost as if that question should be self-explanatory.

"Yes, but I don't care. I just want to stop you," she says, her voice wicked.

Suddenly, I am a zombie. It feels like someone is ripping my face in half—seeing as it is ripped in half. The bone that is revealed to the light burns—as if the light is cooking my skin. Then I realize it is. My skin starts to bubble.

"Now you know what it feels like," she says. Then she starts to swing her now whole arms at me. I can only stand still and do nothing—just like earlier when she couldn't do anything. I'm suddenly lying in a pile of limbs.

Miranda comes up behind Diliah, and says *"Good job, sis."* Then she walks over to me. *"You did this to her,"* her voice begins to fade into another. *"It's only right she does it to you!"* When I look up, I notice that it's not Miranda anymore. It's Blair.

The Novus Proprius Chronicles

Chapter 17

"Zaina, wake up. It's me, B—" I heard someone say. Then I became aware of the things going on around me. First off—I was screaming and I didn't know why. My eye seemed to have healed overnight, even though it still itched a little. Also, Byrd had been shaking me, trying to get me to wake up, until I accidently knocked her out.

When the blurriness had finally faded, I ran over to her. As I sat there, trying to get her to wake up now, the dream came rushing towards me. Gigi, the river, the supposedly Goth Emo girl, the zombie girl, Diliah, and Blair.

After trying to wake her up gently for a few minutes, I decided to resort to the only thing left to try—a bucket of ice cold water. This worked, unfortunately for Byrd but it was entertaining for me. "Remind me next time *not* to try and wake you up," she said, looking at her dripping wet hair that was now clumped up with mud.

"Or better yet—just get Phantom to do it next time," I said with a grin, helping her to her feet.

"Ah, now that sounds like fun," she laughed. "Quick, go back to sleep! I'll go get him," she said playfully as she semi-ran out of the cave's entrance. The she stopped, as if she knew a question was coming. Then I remembered they could read minds and that she would always know what I was going to do.

"What does your soul necklace look like?" I asked, even though she already knew what I was going to say. She pulled out a silver chain and showed it to me.

It was hard to describe. It kind of looked like a compass, but at the same time, it didn't. I looked back down at mine. While hers had a silver chain, mine had a gold one. "Why do you have a silver chain?" I asked, curiously.

"Werewolves are allergic to silver," Byrd explained, trying to say it nice, even though I could tell she was surprised she was explaining this to me.

Then she walked up next to me and said, "Touch it." The second I placed my finger on the cool chain, I pulled it back as it sizzled and bubbled out gooey, red, blood. Never had it occurred to me that I was allergic to anything. I had heard about it, but I had never believed it before. I had always just thought it was just people making up stories. *That would explain why there is no silver around here,* I thought.

After Byrd and I talked, I got ready for school. As it turns out, Byrd had come to wake me up and make sure that I came to school today. *Of course Gigi sent you*, I thought to myself when she'd told me.

While I got ready, I thought about how Cy had told me one day that humans changed their clothes everyday—some even changed them twice a day or more! We never got to change our clothes, but maybe once a month—sometimes the wait was even longer. That was when the butterflies came with crates of supplies. Then it occurred to me; I'd seen butterflies before. Why was I so shocked when I talked to one for the first time?

As this thought ran through my mind, I couldn't help but remember what we had learned in class. The humans were famous for making a lot of clothes. What if they were the ones supplying us with food and clothes, and then they made the butterflies take them to us because we already knew about the butterflies?

I continued brain storming. For some reason, as I was washing my face and an image shot into my head. I was being attacked at school by a butterfly—and I wasn't wearing my necklace. I searched around the cave for the tear drop, yet it remained out of sight. I looked up and Byrd was holding it, swinging it back and forth; the expression on her face made me think that she was thinking really hard about something that might have happened when she was two years old.

"Hey, can I have that back?" I asked cautiously, walking up next to her waving my hand in front of her face. All she did was continue to stare up at the baby blue sky. I gave her a small push.

"Hum?" she asked, as if what I had just said had been lost with the wind that had just recently begun to stir.

I repeated the question, though I was beginning to become restless. She stared down at it as if she had never seen it before.

"Uh," she said this as if she were thinking. "Yeah." This time around, she just sounded disturbed somehow. As she gave back the necklace, it almost felt as if my heart was jumping—like the feelings one gets when they see a person they really like. I wondered if everyone felt like that with their soul necklace.

"Thanks, I think," I said, for some reason, turning the pendant around and around in my hand, inspecting it—

almost like I thought something was wrong with it.

I couldn't figure out why Byrd was acting so strange, but I just knew that it had something to do with Miranda and Diliah. Even though Diliah wasn't necessarily alive, she was still able to be brought back from the dead—if someone could do it once, I was pretty sure they'd do it again.

All though Byrd had been acting weird, she soon snapped out of it. The weirdest part about it is that she didn't remember any of it. Almost as if she had been possessed by some demon. Once we had walked to school together, she stood still by the edge where the tree line stopped. She looked as though she didn't want to get caught for shoplifting or something.

"Bye, I guess." I said, as she rolled her eyes for some reason.

"Mhm," she mumbled as she just walked off; almost as if I was the nerd and she was the popular one.

"Okay then," I muttered almost bitterly. I started walking towards the school when I saw the white blob again. Just as before, all I could make out was a pony tail. Ignoring the blob as best I could, I walked into the school, late as usual.

Once I was in my classroom, I noticed something on my desk. A notebook? No—a diary.

Chapter 18

I looked up at Gigi, who was avoiding eye contact. Then she looked back down at the book she was reading. I looked around the room and noticed Cy was gone. So was Blaze—and Ruby. *Odd*, I thought. The only people in class were Phantom, Bow and I. *This'll be an interesting class period*, I thought.

As I sat down at my desk, I read the cover of the diary. On it stood 'Sylvia's diary. Keep out!' *Wow, kind of extreme don't ya think?* I thought, wondering what she was hiding. As I thought of this, I started thinking about how familiar the name Sylvia was to me.

I looked up at Gigi again and asked, "Am I supposed to read this?"

"Duh," Bow said, annoyed. He seemed oddly amused with intervening in someone else's private life.

"Okay then, gosh," I said, sitting down, picking up the notebook lazily, and beginning to read.

Once it was finally time for lunch, Bow, Phantom and I sat at the table talking about our diaries. "My person kept complaining about how their parents won't let them have a rat and how bad they want one," Phantom complained as if he were hoping for something more interesting.

"Really? My person was talking about crazy water dreams and flying pigs…and cows with gills," Bow recalled, laughing. "It was rather entertaining, but at the same time I think they had some serious social issues."

"My person kept talking about—" then I paused. Maybe Bow and Phantom didn't need to know about the girl Sylvia, and how she was having warning dreams about the apocalypse. She also mentioned Adamè, the witch I'm supposed to save. "Guys." *Guys?* I thought. Seriously? *I couldn't come up with anything better?*

Phantom looked over at me and raised an eyebrow as if asking if that was really what she wrote about. As Bow sat there, trying to eat a big, bloody, juicy steak without getting any blood on his face, I mouthed the words, "I'll tell you later." Then I chomped down into my thick juicy, raw steak as well.

During the rest of class, we were supposed to finish reading the diaries. Unfortunately, I had already finished reading my diary. After all, it was rather short. I guess the plus to being finished was that now I had time to think it all through and process all this information.

The weather, the dreams, the Maltese, the singing, which I thought was especially odd and creepy, and then the French? I wasn't exactly sure where the French came from, or the Maltese thing, but they all seemed like factors to the end of the world; nothing more, nothing less. There was no explanation for it. It was just the end that would lead to the beginning of a new world.

"Gigi, what's a Maltese?" I asked, thinking I might as well do something other then sit around.

"It's a type of dog; the humans had all kinds of breeds because different people liked different types of dogs," she said. She had this odd way of explaining things. When you would ask her a question, she would shake her head up and down as if she were trying to remember something from a past life. That made it all the more obvious that she wasn't just any old teacher. Normally, you would think that she would go look it up in some human text book or something—that's how most of the teachers acted on the island.

"Yum!" Phantom joked, pausing his reading to join our

discussion.

"Ha-ha. Very funny," she said as if she didn't appreciate his sarcasm. "But no, humans kept them as pets," she said, her head bobbing as usual. *Well duh, I kind of guessed that,* I thought, slightly irritated.

"Can you guys shut up?" Bow yelled in a joking way before continuing to read his diary.

After class, I walked outside wondering if I would possibly see the blob. Before it would creep me out, but now I felt comforted by its presence. I didn't know why, though. Every time I saw it, I couldn't help but think that I knew it. I looked around for it, only this time I saw Duke not the blob.

"Hey Zaina, have you seen Giz?" Duke asked, worriedly, as he ran up beside me.

"No, why?" I said, confused, hoping nothing was wrong.

"Well, I haven't seen him since the day after the woods," he explained. He looked extremely worried, which was unusual for this always smiling, showing off his fangs type of person.

"Do you think someone may have hurt him?" I asked, feeling like I was maybe jumping to conclusions. However, I felt like I was reading his mind this time, not the other way around.

"I…don't know," he said, rubbing his temples. Though Duke seemed like a tough guy, I could see tears starting to swell up in his eyes. I could tell him and his brother were close—and not just by blood.

"Well, let's go look for him. I think I know where we can look first," I said, reassuringly. Then we walked off, heading towards that little place where my nightmare had occurred.

The Novus Proprius Chronicles

Chapter 19

As we walked over to Miranda's shop, I explained what had happened the night before—and the dream. I couldn't help but exaggerate the fight. By the time we had gotten to the shop, I had finished telling the story with Duke looking at me funny. I wasn't sure if he was horrified or impressed. It was hard to tell, in spite of all the gore and incredible fighting, he kept a strict poker face.

"That's wonderful," he bluffed. "Now, you did this all by yourself?" he asked, looking at me with an odd look of terror—I hoped he wasn't starting to suspect that I had done something to his brother.

"Yeah?" I said defensively, pausing to look at him. "What? You don't think I can beat a zombie?" I gave him a look that was meant to make him feel bad.

"No, it's not that. It's just, most of the time when someone brings back someone from the dead, there is a specific reason," he said, looking confused.

"Didn't you hear what I said about the dream? She came to kill me!" I said in my defense.

"No, I think that someone is just trying to make you

think that," he said calmingly, trying to explain.

"And why is that?" I said, crossing my arms across my chest. I was beginning to get mad.

"Well, only good witches can bring back the dead. Rebels don't have the power to," he explained though I gave him a look of confusion.

"What are rebels?" I asked, and I could already tell this was going to be a long conversation.

"No one told you?" I shook my head to indicate that no one had told me. He gave a low growl. "Okay. Rebels are witches that use their powers for evil, and when a witch dies all the spells she casted in her life die with her. Another witch will inherit, so to say, these powers. If a Rebel is to get a hold of a good witches' power, they could reverse the spell and use it to harm people—creatures. Whatever. You know what I mean," he explained as short as he possibly could.

"So, let's say a rebel got a hold of Adamè's spells. They could potentially create a new virus, couldn't they?" I asked, worriedly. It was all starting to make sense in my head now.

"Yeah, probably," he said with such sadness I wondered if he blamed himself.

"Maybe that's what's happening! Maybe someone, or a rebel I guess, wants to take control of Adamè's powers to kill the whole earth. I mean, that would happen wouldn't it?" I asked, enjoying this strange epiphany.

He shrugged and said, "I don't know. This is something you'll have to talk to Gigi about." *Ugh, my favorite person of all times,* I thought grimly.

Once we got to the hair salon, we investigated the shop a little. I looked in the girl's bathroom, and the pink dust was gone—like someone had purposely moved the ashes, I guess you could call them.

"Nothing," I said, as Duke came out of the boy's bathroom.

"It's not like he would just fly off to a different island without telling us," he said hopefully glancing around the shop one last time.

"Why wouldn't he? After all, that's what my dad did," I said, kicking up a few locks of hair on the floor with my bare foot.

"I'm sure there's a perfectly good reason for him leaving." He said, trying to comfort me. It wasn't working because I had a feeling he knew more than he was sharing.

"Right, because there is always a good reason for everything, isn't there? If that's true, tell me the wonderful reason for my mom dying," I said, beginning to yell as painful memories of coming home to find my mother dead and my father lying began to surface once more.

I couldn't take it anymore. There was all this anger locked up inside of me, and it needed to come out. I felt like if it didn't come out, I would explode like Diliah's skin had the night before when we were fighting.

It looked like Duke was about to say something, probably something to try and comfort me, but there was a sudden loud gunshot followed by screaming. "What was that?" he yelled, fear almost visible in his tone. Unless Giz screamed like a little girl, I was sure he was fine. Then I thought about something—that scream sounded oddly familiar. It almost sounded like Cy's.

Cyprus

I hear a loud 'pow' sound but the noise wasn't coming towards me. Maybe it was going towards the boy who was next to me. I could tell it was a boy by the way he didn't scream and how he would growl. For a while, I wondered if it was even a werewolf. I heard a voice come from behind me. The voice didn't sound familiar, but there was a certain evil lingering in the depths of it.

"If you don't tell me what you know then I will do the same thing to you that I did to that boy over there," the voice said. I could tell it was a girl. The pitch of her voice was chilling. She seemed like one of the popular girls in school.

"I told you! I don't know anything!" I shrieked, trying to turn around to see who the girl was and who the boy was, but the rope that held me tight was too strong. Then I thought, *is this how I'm going to die?*

"Okay then. We will just have to do it the hard way," she said, sounding almost pleased. The girl opened my eyes to the point where I was starting to wonder if she was going to tear my eye balls out. But what she did was much, much worse. I looked up, still trying to see her face, with no success. Suddenly, I felt a burning hot substance hit my eyes.

I screamed on the top of my lungs, trying to get someone to come and save me—us I mean. Whoever that other boy was. "What is that?" I shrieked, the pain in my eyes consistent and not going away.

"It's called bleach. Humans use it to clean their houses. I'm sure you've read about it," she said mockingly, pouring another glug into my eyes, before letting my eye lids go. I blinked a great deal before I stopped, seeing as blinking only made it worse. I looked around, but all I could see was white blur. *Have I gone blind?* I thought frantically.

"I'm serious! I don't know anything!" I pleaded, hoping this villainous girl would come to my senses.

"Yes well he does, but he won't talk. Maybe you can give him some incentive to?" she said. She must have done something, because I suddenly heard the boy talk.

"Cy! I know you don't know anything! And I'm sorry you have to go through this!" I heard him yell. Just then I realized who the boy was. It was Gizmo.

Duke

I was running as fast as I could to the cave which was

near, but at the same time far away from Zaina's cave. Her story about the zombie girl, Diliah, was incredibly suspicious, but I didn't believe she would ever hurt Giz. And anyways, she was with me. How could she hurt someone if she was with me?

We kept running. By now Byrd had met up with us, midpoint. We would have flown there, but Zaina was right—flying would probably give us away more than if we crept up. But still, we were being way too slow. Eventually, we had reached the cave entrance. It wasn't particularly large, but it wasn't small either. Zaina told me to wait, but I didn't bother to listen. I knew Giz was in there. I needed to help him.

Byrd

What Duke had done was extremely reckless. We were about to find out who we were supposed to stop, as Zaina calls it, and Duke just had to run in. All because of stupid old Gizmo! He was always the one getting the attention. I wouldn't be surprised if he had set this all up himself.

Zaina

I couldn't believe he did that. I needed to know if my suspicion was right. And he just decided running in was a better solution? With no other choice, I ran in behind him. As far as I knew, Byrd had stayed back. I wasn't sure why, though. "Duke?" I whispered as loud as I could before it become a regular sentence.

Duke

I didn't care what Zaina said. I was going to go into this cave. Before I got to the part where I could feel Giz's heart pump slower and slower by the second, I was confronted by another butterfly.

Why would a butterfly work with a rebel? *Oh well*, I thought. That didn't matter. All that mattered was that I needed to go help Giz. I was about to scare it off, when I saw Zaina pounce on it in her wolf form. She bit at its neck as blood spewed out of the side. Zaina seemed to be enjoying this mutilation. Was this a good thing?

She tugged at the beast's neck, and more blood poured out. "Um, Zaina? Can we keep going?" I asked, worriedly.

She looked up at me and grew back to her normal self, even though she was still covered in blood. I'd never seen Rusty this violent. She thought I'd only known her for a couple days, but truth be told—I'd been watching her most of her life. I'd tell her that, if only it wasn't so creepy.

I charged into the room where I could hear Giz's heart pumping. I didn't see anything but two crippled figures lying on the floor. I looked closely and saw that one was, indeed, Giz, but the other one was—Cy?

What did she have to do with any of this? She barely knew anything. I ran over to her and noticed she was fine despite a few bruises, and then I ran over to Giz. He, on the other hand, was dying. And I knew this, but I didn't want to think about it.

Zaina ran over to me. "Go help Cy!" I yelled as I hugged Giz close to me, hoping he would wake up as Rusty tried waking up Cy. The good news was that she did wake up, only she couldn't see anything. She said all she could see was white blurs.

I continued to rock back and forth, Giz lying in my arms. Cy was sitting next to me, her hand on my shoulder and Zaina had gone out to get Byrd. When they returned, Byrd came and sat by me, but she didn't even bother to look at our brother as he slowly died in my arms. I could feel him take in a big breath and then he said something. "Hey," he managed to stutter as he finally awoke.

"Hey 'lil bro," I said, casting a smile down at my dying brother. Byrd still refused to look at him.

"Am I d-d-dy-dying?" he asked as he began coughing up blood. I couldn't help but wonder—could I have saved him if I had gotten here sooner? If only Zaina hadn't wanted to stay and chit chat, then maybe my little baby brother would have had more time.

"No. Of course not. Why would you think that?" I tried to say though I began to cry.

"Um… I-I don-don't know. I ca-can't f-f-feel m-my leg-legs." He mumbled, loosing more and more color in his face as he spoke.

My heart began to break as he started humming the little old Irish lullaby that our mother used to sing to us as we were kids. When our mother had died, he memorized it and every night he would hum it to me when I couldn't sleep.

He hadn't sung it to me in a while. It's too bad this was the last time he ever would.

Memories began to blur in my mind. As he took his last breaths, I remembered the time that he and I made a blood oath. We said that we would always be there for each other, and we would never let anything happen to the other. I felt like such a failure. I couldn't even protect my own little brother from some worthless rebel.

Giz took his last breath and I whispered, "Forever and always shall you lie in my heart. Whether it's the bottom or the top—you will *always* be there," then he was gone. No more life stirred in him. All that was left was a corpse, lying in my arms.

Zaina

Gizmo's death was devastating. Never had I seen Duke this furious. I didn't know Giz too well, myself, but I could feel his older brother's anger pouring out of him like an endless waterfall. Something about the way he was acting made me mourn the loss of Giz as if he were my own brother.

Out of everyone, Cy seemed to be taking it hard because

she felt like she could have helped since she was there when he got shot. I kept trying to tell her that she couldn't have done anything. After all, she didn't know anything.

"But I could have made something up," she would sob every time. Out of everybody, though, Duke blamed himself the most. He kept saying that he should have protected his little baby brother better.

I also think he blamed me since he had to explain to me what rebels were. In a way, we were all to blame. We should have looked out for each other better than we did. Or tried. I mean, if this was all we could do when it came to protecting each other, then we might as well give up now and let the world end.

The funeral was heartbreaking. It must have been a custom at butterfly funerals to talk about things that the deceased didn't want anyone to know. Duke told us all about the blood oath they had made, which was even more proof that he blamed himself. Gigi had come, too. She brought his soul necklace.

"It's too bad you never got to wear it yourself," Gigi said putting the necklace next to him in his red velvet coffin. The pendent was a rose, like Duke's, only it was alive and it had angel wings behind it. "It represents friendship, love, and eternal hope. You would have deserved it," she said, smiling though Byrd just rolled her eyes.

"Yes he would have. He always had a smile for everyone. And he didn't like killing anything. I should have died. Not him." Duke said, looking like he was going to cry again.

The few days before the funeral, that was all he would do. He would sit in a corner, and hug one of Gizmo's old t-shirts. He wouldn't eat anything. He wouldn't talk to anyone. He would just sit and cry. Sometimes he would scream, "Why did you leave me?" while no one was around, but those were truly the only words he'd said before the funeral.

"At least he had a good life," Byrd said, trying to comfort Duke with no success.

Cy stood there, looking for her way to the grave. Blaze came up and helped her. Ever since the cave, she hadn't been able to see anything. I didn't think bleach was all that was done to her eyes.

"I didn't know you very well, but I can tell a good person from a bad person when I see one. You were very sweet that day when we were flying away in the woods. You were the first person who actually said I was beautiful. If you can hear me, then I hope you know that I had high hopes for us," she said, smiling at the memory. Blaze looked down at Giz with jealousy. I didn't know why he would envy a dead boy.

Cy began to ball her eyes out. Of course, it was my turn. I wondered if it was alright refuse to say anything like Byrd had.

I walked up next to him. "Like Cy said, I didn't know you all too well. But you seemed and sound like a great person. Our first impression was a bit odd, but it seems as though that's just how you were." There was a low chuckle that spread through the few of us. Even Duke quietly chuckled, probably remembering something that had happened as a child.

"It's really sad that your life had to end so shortly. But it seems like no matter what you do, someone or something always dies. Whether it's a dream or a friend—something always dies," I said, both to Gizmo and myself. I turned around and looked at the others. "I'm tired of death. Yet I'm expected to save the world," I said, directing myself back at Giz. "Just know that whatever I do next is in honor of your spirit. I wish I could have gotten to know you better." I closed my eyes, and Duke stepped up again.

"You were a great brother. And Zaina is right. You were always a little on the weird side. But so was I, right? Gosh I wish I could hear your voice one more time. I should be in that grave, and if not instead of you, then with you. Trust me. I'll be sure to kill that thing for you," he said hatefully, as he started humming the lullaby that Giz had hummed just the other day, in the cave.

He walked up and closed the coffin's lid. For a second, I was expecting to see Giz sit up and start laughing. But as much as I thought this, nothing happened. When Duke was done humming the song, Gigi raised her hand and the coffin lit on fire.

"May you rest in peace, and have a safe trip to heaven or whatever after life there may be. Let the light guide you there, while I can't," Duke said. He looked down at his hand where a small scar lie—I'd never noticed it before. "I'll see you soon." When he closed his hand and made it into a fist, a tear rolled down his face. As if on cue, it started to rain, as if even the earth was sad to see him go.

Chapter 20

"It would be better if you went," Phantom argued. This discussion had been going on for at least ten minutes now if not more.

"No, I'm going to stay. Cy and Duke need me," I snapped back, again. When was he going to realize that he wasn't going to win?

"Blaze and Byrd can take care of them," he said, seeming utterly annoyed.

"Wait, I thought Byrd was coming with us?" I asked, thinking of the conversation Byrd and I had the other night.

"Well, she said she wanted to stay here," he said as he shrugged lazily. "I guess to take care of Duke or something."

"Oh," I had been looking forward to learning how to fight with her, but I guess not anymore.

"Thanks, I feel the love. I really do," he rolled his eyes and then continued. "Oh, and one more thing; Gigi thinks that I should teach you some basic, defensive witchcraft since we now know that we are dealing with rebels and not wolves or butterflies," he said looking down at his shoes as if he were embarrassed.

"Wait, you know witchcraft?" I asked, raising an eyebrow. *Impressive*, I thought.

"Yeah, Gigi taught me some a while ago," he said with another lazy shrug, only this time, I read it as a threat not a gesture.

"Oh, okay," I said simply, not sure what to think of that.

"So you agree to go to Hollings?" He asked, hopefully.

Hollings, I thought. Supposedly, that was the island that I was supposed to go to, to fight Miranda and also to meet some girl that was supposed to help me do so. It was also the island that Phantom and Ellen had originally moved from. All though, you couldn't trust or believe anyone these days.

"I guess," I said, sadly, realizing I had lost this argument.

"Kay, good," he said, looking relived. His body seemed to loosen up as if he believed he could relax now that I'd agreed.

I went to school one more time before I headed out for

the boats that morning. The sun was in the sky, promising us a warm day on the sea, but thick clouds were threatening the sun right next to it—hoping to overlap it and just barely let any light escape, as if to taunt us with its beautiful rays hidden just out of sight.

"Where are you going, Zaina?" Ruby asked curiously. *Of course she wants to know*, I thought, annoyed.

"I'm not quite sure myself," I said as convincingly as I could. She seemed to believe me—sort of.

"That's wonderful!" Phantom said, winking at me. I just glared at him.

"Yup," I looked around the classroom one more time—for all I knew this could be the last classroom I would ever see. I paused and then eventually said, "Okay well, I really have got to go." I looked around awkwardly.

"Hey Zaina?" Ruby said again. I was surprised Bow hadn't said anything. Blaze was just sitting by the window, glaring at a nearby bush.

"Uh, yeah?" I said, cautiously, switching my weight from foot to foot anxiously.

"You were with that boy—oh, what was his name?" she

asked, as insensitively as I expected she'd be.

"Gizmo," Cy said, blankly. I could tell she was still having trouble with the idea that Giz was dead and she was blind.

"Yeah him. You were with him when he died, weren't you?" she looked at me and gave me a devilish smirk as if she thought all of this was a game.

"Yeah. I was with him," I said guiltily, staring down at my shoes and messing around with my finger nails.

"How did he die?" she said as sweetly as if we were talking about puppies.

"You know, I really need to get going! Bye everyone," I said, awkwardly, not wanting to answer the question. Ruby just looked up at me, confused and slightly angry.

"So what? You're not going to answer the question?" she asked as if she deserved all the answers in the universe.

"She doesn't need to!" Gigi snapped as scolded her with her eyes.

"Pish posh," she said, rolling her eyes. Before I ran out the door, I hurried over to Cy and gave her a hug.

"I'll be back soon." I said as reassuringly as I could. She simply nodded. "I promise…" I said, not sure if I was trying to convince her or me.

That seemed like a lie to me. I wasn't even sure if I was going to survive. And even if I did, I wasn't sure Gigi would let me come back. The other day she was talking about my 'noble obligations' and how they were all in Hollings.

* * *

"This will probably be a little bit bumpy for the most part," Phantom said. A little after I had gotten to the boat, Gigi and Phantom had appeared out of thin air. It was around lunch time now.

"We dismissed class early," Gigi said happily, seeming relieved.

"What? Were they getting on your nerves?" I asked sarcastically. As if I actually had to ask that.

"Yes. Ruby kept complaining that you didn't answer her question," she twisted her face into a scowl as she stared over at a big chest on the boat. *Wow*, I thought, *my first time on a boat*.

"Is everything okay?" I asked as I followed her gaze to the box.

"I think so. Well, it depends if Phantom here grabbed everything," she said as she gave Phantom a scowl similar to the one she had given the box.

"I grabbed everything that you said, I think," he started rubbing the back of his neck nervously.

"How much ya wanna bet you forgot something?" I said, smirking even though you could tell Phantom didn't find it that funny himself.

"Ha-ha, very funny," he said anxiously, following Gigi over to the chest.

She looked into it, and yelled, "Ha!" making us both jump back. "I knew it. You forgot the sword!" She said it like it mattered a great deal.

"But you said I should teach her some witchcraft. Not sword fighting," he said defensively. I just sat there, looking back and forth at the two of them arguing.

"That doesn't mean that she won't need to know it," she scolded like an old woman angry with her grandchild for stealing something.

"Ugh, then what do you propose we do? Hum?" he asked stubbornly. *Time to but in*, I thought.

"Hey? Why don't you guys just buy a new sword?" I proposed. They both just looked at me like I had mentioned suicide.

"You obviously don't understand that this sword is very special and worth a lot of money," Gigi said, straightening up.

"Then go out and buy a sword that looks like it. Then you can skip around like a magical pixie pony and tell everyone it's special or whatever," I said. Phantom chuckled, even though you could tell he regretted it afterwards.

"It doesn't work that way," she said, angrily. *Oh, I see how it is. It is probably magically enchanted or something*, I thought. "Phantom?" she almost yelled a tad.

Phantom, who had been rubbing his head trying not to laugh at my stupidity, looked up and said, "Hum?"

"Go to my house and grab it," she said as the boat rang its bells, letting us know that we would be leaving soon.

"I'll never make it back to the boat in time," he said pitifully.

"Don't run, fly," she said simply as if it were a commonly known fact that suddenly Phantom could sprout wings.

"Fly? Phantom can fly?" I asked, in astonishment as I watched him nod, sprout wings and flying away as if he did it all the time. They looked like butterfly wings, but his body didn't change. He just looked like himself.

"Yeah. He didn't tell you he was a banshee?" Gigi said, as we both stared at the blob flying as fast as a bullet.

"I'm sorry a ban-what?" I asked, completely confused. This was too much. Giz was dead. Cy was blind. And Phantom was a banshee? That made me wonder what else I was missing. Hey, maybe Blaze was really a girl.

"A banshee," she said it like it was the simplest thing to accept. "Do you know what a banshee is?"

"Uh, no. Am I supposed to?" I asked, with a slight attitude.

"Well, it could be useful," she said, seeming almost a little annoyed herself.

"Well then what are they?" I asked anxiously though I wasn't sure I wanted to know myself.

"Okay, a banshee is someone of one species and then they get bit by a different species and the two genes mix together. If it weren't for me, Tom would be crazy. That's what usually happens," she said self-righteously.

"Wait, how did he become a banshee?" I asked, my brain about to implode from confusion. I hated all these new species I needed to learn.

"Well, he was annoying Duke one day when they were hunting in the woods and Duke bit him," she said, sounding amused. I remembered what Duke had said that day while we were flying. *So Phantom was the werewolf he bit*, I thought comically.

"Oh my gosh," I said, faking surprise. Now knowing they'd known each other for a long time made sense and answered so many questions.

"Yup, Tom's the reason butterflies and wolves aren't supposed to hang out. They're worried it might happen to someone evil. I'm sure you know what I mean. Someone with the wrong intensions could easily become very dangerous," she explained with a look of fear on her face as if this were a serious issue.

"Is that why you look out for Phantom so much? And why you taught him magic?" I asked, wondering so many things.

"I guess. But yeah, that's why he calls himself Phantom instead of Tom. He thinks he's not supposed to be alive," she shrugged. "Which I guess in a way is true. I'm not saying he should die or anything," she said, jokingly. "When Duke decided that he was going to stay behind, he became your shadow. I hope he teaches you well!" she exclaimed, happily.

Before I could ask what a shadow was, Phantom was back. These past few days, I learned what rebels and banshees were. I hadn't quite learned what a shadow was but I was sure I would. All this was making me feel incredibly left out. "Oh hey Tom. I was just explaining to Zaina what you are," she smiled sweetly. He smiled back, but I could tell it was fake.

"Great," he said, faking joy. Just as he got on the boat, it took off. Like Phantom said, it was most definitely going to be bumpy.

Later, when I got a chance to actually look at the sword, I could tell why Gigi wanted it so bad. Not only was it the coolest thing I'd ever seen, it was also beautiful. It looked like a mix between a pirate sword and a broad sword. It had emeralds embedded on the handle, and down the left side of it. The green looked absolutely mesmerizing against the gold colored iron.

For the first couple hours, Phantom didn't feel like training me since the ride was so bumpy, or so he said. So we talked instead. "Hey Phantom?" I asked as I felt like a little kid, venturing for the truth.

"Yeah?" he mumbled, looking up at me. I hope I didn't wake him up, seeing as how he was just lying on the deck, blocking the sun out of his eyes.

"Gigi said you were my shadow?" I asked, hoping he would explain. This seemed like something that I really needed to know.

"Ha," he started, as if knowing I had no clue what she was talking about once again. "A shadow is someone in a prophecy. For example, you are the character—the one that the prophecy is about. The shadows, being me, Byrd, and the girl I was telling you about, are the ones that help you—or the character," he said, sounding annoyed. I wouldn't be surprised if he would be happy if our places were switched—I wouldn't mind either.

"Let me guess, you wish you were the character, or whatever it's called?" I asked, hoping my intuition was correct and my questions not misplaced.

He shrugged and said, "I wouldn't put it like that." He had a mean glare on his face, though I couldn't tell if it was because of the sun in his eyes or the topic.

"I'm right, aren't I?" I asked, prodding for the truth. He just shrugged again and looked down at his hands. "Don't you lie to me," I warned, jokingly.

"Let's just say—people don't pay as much attention to me—as I would like, I guess," he said, looking embarrassed.

"Wow, Phantom. Your wimpy-ness surprises me sometimes," I joked, though he just rolled his eyes, and shrugged as usual.

Then suddenly, all the little 'oh my gosh, you're so stupid' eye rolls and laughs at each other's humiliation was replaced with visions of blood and fire. It's one thing to be envied yet another thing to be hated.

"Whatever," he said angrily, scowling at me from across

the deck.

"Hey, what's wrong?" I asked, walking over trying to comfort him.

"Nothing," he said, pushing my hand away as I tried to lay it on his shoulder. "Let's just get started with training."

"Nope," I said stubbornly, crossing my arms across my chest, as if to symbolize my stubbornness.

"What? Why?" he asked. The hatred was gone and replaced with annoyance.

"I am not doing anything until you tell me what's wrong," I said as if I were an irritating younger sibling who wanted something they couldn't have.

"Ugh, you—you're so," he said as he clawed at his face. "stubborn! Why are you so stubborn?" he spat plainly as I shrugged with a daredevil grin.

"I get it from my mom and dad," I began, trying not to think too much about my parents. "I take it back; I get my stubbornness from my mom and my laziness from my dad," I finished.

"Dad's not lazy," Phantom blurted out. Suddenly, I realized what he had said, as he covered his mouth comically.

"Yes he is. Wait—you know my dad?" I asked, confused. *People need to come clean and tell me everything they know*, I thought, feeling lied to.

"That's not important. Now, we really need to work on training," he said enthusiastically, trying to change the subject.

"Fine," I said with a loud sigh. He simply looked relived until I said, "but you still haven't told me why you're upset." He just sighed in miserable failure.

"Zaina, just do some training and then bug him later," Gigi suddenly said, appearing out of nowhere. Had she been eavesdropping?

"Yeah Zaina," Phantom said, standing up and folding his arms across his chest as if he had never acted like a jealous toddler.

"Phantom. Do I need to get someone else to train her?" Gigi said, quite stubbornly herself.

"No, it's fine. Zaina, here, just needs to learn that I am the one who is in charge," he said, matching Gigi and my stubbornness.

"Oh, so this is my fault now, is it?" I asked, feeling rather angry. I was always getting blamed for things I hadn't done.

"Uh, no?" Phantom said, looking more like Ruby then someone who was supposed to train me for war.

"But that's what you just said," I pointed out, hoping he felt helpless.

"So, I didn't mean it like that…or something," he just shook his head indicating that he had no idea what he was talking about.

"What?" I asked, confused. This conversation was going nowhere.

Before Phantom could reply, Gigi yelled, "It doesn't matter. Just start training." Though Phantom mimicked Gigi's words, he did as he was told.

First, Phantom gave me something made out of leather. He called it a bracer. He said it was to protect my arm from the rope. Only later did I realize he was talking about archery. He handed me the bracer, and I attempted to put it on. It wasn't the putting on that was so frustrating. It was the tying.

"Here; let me help you with that." Phantom said, seeming amused. I just rolled my eyes as he tied the thin leather strips into a neat little bow.

"Thanks," I mumbled when he had finished, not appreciating his help but glad that the bracer was finally on.

"Okay, so this is a Mongolian Hunting Bow," he said, picking up a bow and handing it to me. As I held it in my hands, I couldn't help but realize how much it looked like a backwards three. But instead of the tips curling in, they curled up and out.

I held it up, and pulled the string back. People always made it look so simple—they put the arrow in, pull the string back, aim in about two seconds, release and voila. They shot their target. For me, pulling the string back and keeping my arm steady was hard enough. Phantom, seeing as he was probably reading my mind since he was part butterfly, simply laughed.

"Here, let me see it for a second," he said, holding his hand out, expecting me to give him the bow even though I had no intention of doing so.

I looked down at his hand and then down at the bow a

few times before eventually saying, "Nah, I'm good." He just raised his eyebrow and laughed.

"Fine then. I'll just watch you die when you face the rebels," he said, as my mouth dropped; kind of on purpose but at the same time in surprise. "Yup. And I'm going to laugh the whole time." This time, I gave him the evil look and growled.

"Fine," I said, feeling rather grumpy as I threw the bow at him. He lunged at it, as if it would shatter if it even touched the floor.

"Gosh, you didn't have to throw it," he said, cradling the bow in his arms.

"Oh hush it before I take it back. Then you'll never get it again," I said wickedly.

"Yeah, like you could really get it from me," he said, as if it were an invitation. *You better watch what you say,* I thought.

"What is that supposed to mean?" I asked, wondering where all this constant bickering was coming from.

"Um, I don't know," he said, bluffing—I could tell.

"Just that I'm stronger than you," he put simply.

"Yeah right," I argued. *Wow, we really sound like three year olds arguing over dolls,* I thought, annoyed at both Phantom and myself.

"You wanna bet?" he said, playfully. Just to be a show off, he took the bow and pulled the string back, as if he was pulling a blade of grass apart. His arm didn't shake or quiver. It held perfectly still.

"Okay, fine," I said, a bit of humiliation attempting to hide inside my voice. "You can hold your arm still, but can you aim?" This time, humiliation was replaced with rebelliousness. Knowing Phantom, he would take the challenge.

"See, that's what I was getting ready to teach you," he said as he picked up a neon orange arrow. "Do you always have to jump ahead?" he asked.

"What's that supposed to mean?" I asked, defensively. There were so many things he was saying that angered me at that point.

"Exactly what I said," he said, pulling the bow's string back. "Now, watch and learn," he said slowly, licking his lips as he put his eye up next to the string. He aimed at the target that appeared out of nowhere. After maybe half a minute, figures he'd have to take that long to aim, he let go, and hit the target dead set in the middle. I couldn't help myself so I clapped.

"Wow. Still doesn't mean you're stronger though," I said as I held my hand out, telling him with my eyes that I wanted to shoot next.

"Ha, well if you think that was impressive, just wait till you see Witchney shoot!" he said, with admiration in his voice. I could tell he was very impressed by her. Witchney was the girl that was supposed to help steal my crowning glory. As if I couldn't defeat a few rebels on my own.

"Well, the question is—does she aim faster than you?" I smirked, as I pulled the bow string back and aimed.

"Ha-ha, very funny. But yeah, she aims way faster than me," he said, looking slightly embarrassed.

As he finished speaking, I let go of the string. Staring at the target, I noticed that it hadn't hit the target at all; in fact, it flew off the boat and hit something in the water.

"Um, you are going out to get that," Phantom said, wide-eyed, looking at the bloody water.

"Why? Can't you do some magical something or other

to get it out?"

"Ugh, always have to make things difficult, don't you?" He raised his hand and made a small hand gesture, as if waving towards him, and the arrow came flying out of the water; a fish speared through the center of it.

"I was totally aiming for that," I said sarcastically as Gigi walked down to the lower deck where we were training. I didn't want her to think I was incompetent or anything.

"Oh look, a fish," she said, as if she had never seen one before.

"Yeah," Phantom said nodding up and down as if my talents for missing targets were useless.

"Who shot it?" she asked, seeming impressed. She obviously had just missed my mistake.

"I did!" I said, jumping up and down. I did so purposely because I could tell it was getting on Phantom's nerves.

"Good job. Now we have something else to eat," Gigi said happily as she took the fish and walked back to the upper deck.

"Ha-ha!" I said, sticking my tongue out at Phantom. "Ya

know, I'm gonna start calling you Tom," I said. I took another arrow out of the bag, aimed, and missed again.

"Why?" he said, seeming utterly disgusted by this fact.

"'Cause, I can tell it makes you mad," I said, as I walked over to the railing to retrieve the arrow.

"Oh thanks. I can feel the love," he said, as he always did. I aimed again, my arms shaking. Feeling weak, somehow, I lowered the bow.

"So, why do you go by Phantom? I mean, what's so wrong with Tom?" I asked, as I turned back around to look at him.

"I thought Gigi already went over this with you," he said, looking down at the deck floor. "I really shouldn't be alive. And besides, I don't like the name Tom. It sounds too serious," he said as he pulled out a sword. I noticed it wasn't the special one he had flown to go get earlier. This one just looked like a simple training sword.

I put down the bow and said, "So where's my sword?" He just laughed. *Why is he laughing?* I thought frantically, thinking of all the things that could possibly go wrong.

"You're not getting one," he said wickedly as he swung

the metallic sword at my head. Just before the metal and I clashed, I ducked.

"What are you trying to do? Kill me?" I yelled, feeling quite terrified, ducking from another fierce swing.

"No, but it's a thought," he said wickedly, this time swinging at my feet.

"What? How is this training?" I yelled as I jumped. He just laughed; swinging at my stomach this time. I backed up, missing the blade by an inch.

"I'm teaching you how to avoid dying. Ya know, just in case you fight a rebel some other time and you don't have a weapon," he explained, still with a vicious grin. I simply moaned as he swung at my head once again.

Instead of ducking, I arched my back into a somewhat graceful backbend. Just then I realized that the railing was the only thing keeping me up. Just as this alarming thought ran through my mind, the railing vanished, due to one if Phantom's infuriating hand flicks. How was he doing all this? I frantically waved my arms in the air, trying to keep my balance with no success. I screamed and Phantom laughed as I plunged backwards into the frigid sea.

"Never try doing a backbend," Phantom yelled as the boat kept going forward and I continued to struggle in the water. I tried yelling something, but the water was just too cold. The waves crashed over my head and I could feel the ocean attempting to pull me under—with success. My lungs felt like they had bricks in them, and my vision started to get blurry. After a while, everything went black.

Not long after my vision was almost completely blacked out, Phantom was pulling me out of the water, wings out, dangling me by my arms. I was surprised he hadn't tried pulling me out by my hair. Within seconds, I was being dropped onto the deck like a rag doll. He circled up ahead, and landed gracefully onto the deck without a sound.

Looking at him like this made him look somewhat intimidating. His eyes had gone from a crystal blue to a blood red that filled his entire eyes, where only the pupil remained black. Truth be told, if I was to confront a demon, I would imagine its eyes like this. His hands were now accompanied by thick, razor sharp claws. He had fangs almost longer than Duke's. He changed back to normal, once he sat next to me as my teeth chattered together from the icy blue water.

"Okay, I want you to concentrate on being dry and

warm," he said, calmingly. Despite the fact that I was probably dying from pneumonia, I managed to glare at him. "Trust me," he said as if sensing my reluctance. I did as he said, and closed my eyes. "Good. Now imagine someone putting a towel around you and you being dry and warm, dry and warm, dry and warm."

His words echoed through my head, but eventually all I could hear was the sheer, sweet sound of the ocean's waves crashing against the side of the boat. I kept repeating the words in my mind; dry and warm, dry and warm, and a soft, cozy towel wrapping its warm, familiar, woven arms around me. Eventually, my teeth stopped chattering, my hair stopped dripping, and my lips returned to their usual fleshy color. I opened my eyes and suddenly realized—I was dry.

"Holy crap!" I said, jumping up in surprise.

"Congrats! Your first official and successful magic trick," he said as he clapped and laughed, seeming surprisingly proud.

I walked over to where Phantom was now standing and kicked him in the shin. "What did you do that for?" I yelled. While most people would have winced in pain from my kick,

Phantom just chuckled, rubbing his shin as if to try and make it feel better.

"What? Dropping you onto the deck like that or technically throwing you off the boat?" he asked, making me remember all the times people had worked their way around an answer they didn't want to explain.

"Both!" I said, crossing my arms across my chest; I was really grumpy now. *You almost killed me,* I thought, angrily, hoping he could hear me.

"It's all part of the lesson. Don't ever try doing a backbend in a fight. Trust me. It won't do you any good. Besides, people in movies do it just to make themselves look cooler," he said as he flicked his hand to make the boat railing returned. "And anyways; I have my reasons," he finished, shrugging as if he had no reason to explain.

"Okay then," I thought, still upset. *What are movies?* I thought.

"Movies are basically like plays but they are on a big screen," he replied to my unspoken question. "Plus they are cooler and recorded." He shrugged. Then he picked up two swords. *At least I get one this time,* I thought, hopefully. He tossed the other sword to me and I just barely caught it.

"Ya know, this mind reading thing is really starting to get on my nerves," I said, holding up my sword to let him know I was ready.

"Well, you'll just have to deal with it," he replied, swinging his sword at my face. I blocked it and both our swords clashed, creating sparks that seemed to flow down like tiny parachutes.

"Remember. Your best bet at survival when your opponent is coming at you from above would be to run. But seeing as you're extremely stubborn you probably won't do that 'cause I told you to do so," he said as he waved his sword high in the air and the sun's rays reflected off of it, nearly blinding me.

Before he hurled the thing down onto my head, I said, "You're right. I would do this," I said.

For a second, he shot me a confused looked as I ducked down onto my hands, swung around in a 360° circle, and knocked him down onto his back as if he were the rag doll this time. I got back up and put my sword to his throat. "How's that for not strong enough?" I asked mockingly.

"Impressive," was all he said. He got up, after I refused moving the sword away, and then whipped sweat from his forehead. *I think he's nervous*, I thought. *I'm not nervous.* I chuckled lightly.

"I am not nervous," he said as if he had poison bubbling up in the back of his throat. Almost as if he really did think he was stronger than me.

"Yeah, whatever," I said before attacking this time. He just rolled his eyes, which by now I had accepted as a typical 'Phantom action' as he blocked the fierce swing.

After about half an hour of basically running around in circles, blocking and swinging, Phantom somehow managed to cut my other leg open. However, it was only because I was off guard getting a drink of water, and he wasn't supposed to attack then.

"So what? Are you going to teach me how to dress a wound?" I asked; my pride about three centimeters tall. Maybe even smaller.

"No, I'm going to teach you how to heal yourself and others," Phantom said, stuttering a tad at the end.

"By others I'm guessing you mean you?" I asked menacingly.

"Unfortunately," he said, sighing afterwards.

"Hey, can I cut you? I mean to heal you of course!" I said sarcastically.

"Uh," he stuttered. "Look. We'll see later. Let's just focus on your leg," he said, looking down at my open wound, which was spewing out blood despite the fact that it wasn't even a deep cut. My right leg was still wrapped up, but by now it had gone numb—which was probably a bad thing.

"What happened to your other leg, anyway?" he asked with curiosity and concern battling in the midst of his voice.

"Well, something with a dream. That's also how I got that tear on my stomach—or was it my ribs? Or both?" I would have looked through the rip in my shirt but Gigi had magically fixed it with her mind.

"That doesn't really matter." He poked the bandage that was covered in a mix between blood and pus. "Does that hurt?"

"Nope," I said, surprised to find out he was somehow touching my leg; I couldn't feel a thing. The bandage had gone from cloth to rock.

"This is bad," he said frantically; standing up, ready to start pacing. "Maybe we should get Ember to heal you."

"Ember?" I asked. *Isn't that the girl, Sylvia mentioned in her diary?* I thought.

"Crap, I meant Gigi," he said, covering his mouth as if he had cursed the gods.

"Oh. Um? What's so wrong with me knowing that?" I asked, wondering what was wrong with her first name. *Of course*, I thought. It all made sense now. Sylvia wrote that some weird girl named Ember came up to her and said she was a witch and that she had paranormal powers. Why didn't I see it before?

"I don't really know," he said, staring up at the sky as if he were deep in thought. "Anyways, we need to get Gigi to heal that for you," he finished, pointing at the cast as if it were some kind of disease.

"Why don't I try to do it, smart one?" I asked; he looked at me as if he had just witnessed a murder. Then his face softened and he began to nod.

"Well, I guess you can try," he said, making the statement sound like an insult to me.

"What? You don't think I can do it?" I asked as he simply shrugged. "Whatever. Just tell me what I need to do," I asked, feeling angry again. I hated it when people lacked faith in me.

He screwed his face into a scowl as if he had just made a swarm of horse flies mad. "First, we should take off the bandage," he said. He flicked his hand this way and that, and eventually the bandage was barely open—but hardly removed. By now the blood and pus had created a cast nearly impossible to break through.

"Hold on. I think I'm gonna need some extra help." He said, walking over to the chest. He got out the special sword—which might I add was extremely sharp—and another, more dull sword. He looked at the two, and in the end decided that the special sword would be better.

"Do you wanna do it or should I?" He asked. I just shrugged. Really the only thing I could feel now was a warm, almost cozy comfort. Almost as if my leg had never gotten hurt, and the cast surrounding it was a wool blanket.

"I don't care," I said, poking the impenetrable cast. "You pick." This was actually kind of entertaining.

"Why don't you do it?" he said. What was supposed to be a suggestion had turned out to be more of a command.

"Oh joy," I said, taking the sword from him. Holding it, I immediately felt tough—and strong. I sawed at the bandages as red and yellow powder puffed out the sides. Not only was I tough, but so was this cast.

When I had finally managed to saw through layers of dried blood and hardened pus, I pried the thing off—a shriek of surprise from me and a foul smell from my leg accompanying this action. The smell was a mix of rotten eggs, mold and exposed bone.

I looked down, in shock, at the little bit of my leg I still had. Half the flesh had molded onto the bandage, meaning when I pulled the cast off, I also pulled off helpless dead skin and flesh with it. Phantom and I stared down in horror as more meat fell onto the deck. Truth be told, my leg looked as if it belonged to a leper, not to myself.

"I—I—I'm gonna be sick!" Phantom shrieked as he ran over to the side of the boat and barfed up half-digested raw steak from lunch.

"You feel sick? I'm the one with a bone leg," I cried,

trying to get up, in the end only losing more flesh.

"You seriously can't feel anything?" he asked in astonishment, wiping vomit from his mouth.

"No," I said, impatiently. When was he finally going to help me heal my leg?

"Okay. Let's just focus on healing you— I'm going to puke again!" he covered his mouth. Indeed, he looked over the side of the boat and barfed up nothing, seeing as he had already barfed up his lunch.

I just rolled my eyes. "Okay. What do I do?"

"Hold on. I think I'm going to need some water," he said selfishly.

"Water? Half my leg is lying on the deck," I said angrily, hoping he would come to his senses.

"You're right," he said. I wonder if he was trying to kill me. If I were to sit here any longer, I would probably die of blood loss. "Okay. Imagine your leg the way it used to be, ya know… before it got all ew-ish." I nodded. "Now close your eyes and tell yourself that you never got hurt in the first place."

I did as he said, and eventually the warm comfort went away and my leg actually felt kind of cold. "Now open your eyes," Phantom finished, stating the obvious.

When I looked down, I saw that my body had created new skin and flesh, yet there still remained a large scar where the original cut had been. The other side's cut had completely vanished, not even leaving a ghost of a scar in its place.

Then I wished that my parents could both be here to be the ones that taught this all to me. But as much as I tried to convince myself that at least my mom was here with me now I just couldn't. It was like this sweet image was blocked by some invisible force field that wished nothing more than pain and agony upon my life. Almost like that force field was my brain not believing she was dead. But she was and I needed to accept that. Then I thought, *why did you leave me, too, Mom?*

"Hey guys? Dinner is ready," Gigi yelled from the top deck.

"I'm not so sure I can eat," Phantom said, staring down at the cast.

I picked it up and said, "I'll go ask Gigi what she wants

me to do with this." I started to walk up to the top deck, where there was the pleasant smell of cooked fish and lemon seasoning, instead of dead meat, lingering in the air.

"Wait, you can get rid of it. Magically I mean," he said hopefully. He was looking down at the cast as if it were a dead body. I guess in a way it was.

"Okay, tell me what to do, oh dear teacher of mine," I said, sarcastically. I put it down next to the pile of meat that was lying on the deck where I had been sitting just a few moments ago.

"Do what you've been doing! Imagine it the way it should be." He almost seemed annoyed.

I did what I was told. I closed my eyes and imagined the cast as a bouquet of flowers, the pieces of flesh as pieces of candy and the blood as just regular water. I could have made it all vanish, but where was the fun in that?

"Abracadabra!" I yelled as everything turned into, indeed, what I had imagined it to be.

"Any respected witch would not yell abracadabra," he rolled his eyes and picked up what was now candy.

"Why?" I asked as I picked up the bouquet of flowers

for Gigi.

We started walking up to the top deck as Gigi answered for Phantom, "Because most witches don't say anything when they cast spells. Plus only rebels chant. You wouldn't want to be mistaken for one of them. Trust me." I just shrugged as I got a plate and was dished a giant, juicy fish from the cook that must have been working on the boat. They obviously didn't understand sarcasm.

"Plus, most witches wouldn't be able to come up with a spell that rhymes that quickly," Phantom said, thinking he was funny. Gigi and I just rolled our eyes as we sat and ate our dinner.

The Novus Proprius Chronicles

Chapter 21

After dinner, Phantom explained to me that he was going to postpone any further 'witch training' as he called it, because he thought I was ready for the rebels. Truth be told, I thought he wasn't training me anymore because he wanted me dead. After our little chat, if that's what you wanted to call it, I went to bed on Gigi's order and Phantom stayed on deck.

The inside of the cabin was small. There was one twin sized bed with lavender pillows and a blanket that had daisy yellow and darker purple stripes. Not the colors I would have picked but it worked I guess. The curtain that was over the small, circular window facing east was more of a butter-yellow. The walls were a neat tan, as if all the other mixed matched colors in the room didn't already throw off your vision enough. There was a light brown colored desk sitting near the door, and that was all that could fit in the bitty room.

I took two steps and had managed to get from the door to the bed. I stood there, debating for a few minutes whether or not I wanted to sleep in the bed and mess up the neat sheets—in the morning I would have to fix them again. I was a bit scared, to be honest. I had never slept in a bed before. All my life I had slept on my little straw mattress by the fire.

I poked the mushy box thing, afraid to lose my finger in all the fluffiness. It was almost too soft for my taste. Eventually, I lied down and sunk into the mattress—it was like lying on a cloud. I wasn't sure if I loved it or hated it. *Deal with it*, I thought. Not long after I told myself this, I fell into a deep, dreamless sleep.

When I woke the next morning, I noticed that the bed was positioned so that the sun would stream into your face as it rose. As much as I hated the extreme mushiness of the mattress, I also hated the thought of getting up. After I sat there for about ten minutes staring into the sun's rays aimlessly, I finally got myself to get up and, unfortunately, fix the bed.

I walked out onto the deck and found Gigi, or Ember, staring out at the ocean. I walked up next to her, but she seemed too immensely concentrated on the lifeless water to notice me. "Hey?" I said, after about five minutes of staring.

"Hum?" she asked, tearing her eyes away from the beautiful sea.

"I said hey," I said once more, wondering where her thoughts had taken her.

"Oh, hey," she said, before returning her concentration to the big blue.

"What are you looking at?" I asked, trying to find what she seemed so interested in.

"Nothing," she said simply. I glanced at her, a confused look printed on my face. "I'm thinking."

"Oh. About what?" I asked, realizing just how nosey I was.

"You," she said, glancing at me sideways.

"That's creepy," I said, awkwardly. She simply chuckled under her breath.

"I'm just thinking about what's going to happen after you and Witchney kill…Miranda," she said, hesitating. The way she said her name made it seem as if she felt bad for her, though she killed Giz. She could never be forgiven for a murder like that.

"What's wrong?" I asked, hatred bubbling up in the

back of my throat at the thought of the person who killed Gizmo.

"I don't know. I just have this weird feeling that we're missing something," she said as she started rubbing her head as though she had been thinking all night. Knowing her, she probably had been. "It just doesn't make sense. I mean—all the prophecies stated that it was someone younger than Miranda. Someone not too much older then you. Someone you wouldn't expect."

"Well, whoever it is, I'll be ready to kill them. Someone that can do that kind of damage without even blinking deserves to die and rot in hell," I said, bitterly. Now the hatred had started boiling over and coming from my mouth the way water would from a pot.

"Spoken like a true friend. I can tell Cy and Giz meant a lot to you," Gigi said, pride shining through her smile.

"They did," I said, thinking about Cyprus. She just smiled and returned her gaze to the ocean, where a speck of land seemed to be coming into view.

"Ah! We're almost there," she said as if she were a child visiting the pet store to look for a potential puppy.

As we got closer and closer, I noticed the lack of abundant trees like we had back home. Really, what I was looking at was a big, vast, treeless field of light colored dirt. Beyond the nothing, there were numerous buildings and brightly colored boxes on wheels. There were also tons of houses; some looked like Gigi's, but some were bigger—some more quaint.

I got off the boat and walked out onto the dirt that seemed so much dryer then the damp, moist dirt back home. As I continued walking, clouds of dust gathered around my bare feet. "You're going to need some shoes," Gigi recommended.

"Some what?" I asked as I shot her yet another baffled look.

"Shoes. The things normal, civilized people wear on their feet," she explained—a hint of impatience in her voice.

"Um, okay?" I shot Phantom a baffled look as well, as if to ask if he knew what she was talking about. In truth, Phantom seemed like an older brother to me—we fought like cats and dogs sometimes yet at the same time we understood each other.

"I'm sure Witch can help you out when it comes to clothes. That is, as long as you don't mind black," he said, and I shot him another baffled look. I was starting to get a headache from all this new information. "She's Goth," he informed me. Then I wondered if, maybe, Witchney was the girl in my dream.

"Well, it would help if we got there," I said stubbornly, wondering when I would get a chance to cool off my burning feet.

"Touché," Phantom grinned. "Guess how we're going to get there," he said wickedly.

"Oh great. We're going to fly aren't we?" I asked, cautiously. After my not so graceful landing the last time I flew, I wasn't looking forward to flying again.

"Oh heck no! You two are too heavy," he said. For a second, I couldn't tell if he was being sarcastic or not.

"What? Are you saying we're fat?" I asked rebelliously. All the while, Gigi was just watching in amusement.

"Maybe," he said guiltily. All three of us laughed. This time we all knew he was joking. He knew better then to make fun of me and Gigi. "Nope, we're driving."

"Driving?" I asked, utterly confused.

"Yup," he began, flicking his hand as one of the boxes on wheels appeared in front of us. This box was target red. "By car," he finished.

Phantom was a surprisingly good driver. As far as I knew, this was his first time driving—or so he said. I was surprised he was even a witch. Deep down inside, I was convinced he was secretly a rebel.

By the time we got to Witchney's house, it was nearly lunch time. I got out of the car and stared at the tan/yellow house with blue shutters standing in front of me. It wasn't huge, but it wasn't small either. Then I noticed something—all the other houses had either black or red shutters. This house had baby blue. "They painted them," Phantom explained.

"What?" I questioned him; my headache was getting worse.

"The shutters. You were thinking about how weird it was that their shutters are blue," he said, making me very annoyed. Once again he was invading on my privacy. Whatever happened to looking into one's eyes?

We walked up to the door where a rather interesting mat lay. It said "Wipe your paws!"

I read it and said, "That is so not funny." Phantom laughed and rang the doorbell. A woman with frizzy, fire red hair and a tan made of freckles answered.

"Phantom?" she said with a hint of alarm in her voice.

"What are you doing here?" She almost seemed mad.

"Sorry, Mrs. Traps," he said, pointing at me. "This here is a good friend of mine, and she is here to speak with Witch." She seemed even madder when he referred to Witchney as 'Witch'.

"Does this friend have a name?" she asked, not seeming pleased but not unfriendly either.

"My name is Zai—" I began, though before I could finish, Phantom interrupted.

"Zosia! Don't you just love that name?" he exclaimed. I gave him a look that was mixed between confusion and anger.

"Of course I do. That's the name of her Witchney's sister," Mrs. Traps announced.

Phantom began to rub his head and said, "Ugh, can we come in? I'll explain everything in there."

"Of course," she said as if she had just been insulted.

Once we got inside, Mrs. Traps showed me to a door where loud music was playing on the other side. She told me Witchney was in there—meanwhile, she and Phantom argued things over in the kitchen. I knocked on the door cautiously. The music stopped and I heard a very annoyed sounding voice say, 'what now' almost as if I really was the Zosia Phantom had, for some reason, named me after.

"Um, hi? My name is Zaina. Are you—" I said, cautiously, though before I could finish, the door swung open.

In the door way stood a girl that was about five inches shorter than me—and I was pretty short to begin with. She had beautiful silky red hair, unlike her mom's, yet the baby blue eyes they shared. Another thing Witchney and her mother didn't share was the freckles. While her mom was spotted like a Dalmatian, Witch remained a blank sheet of paper. Indeed, she was the girl in my dream.

"Oh, crap. You're here so soon," she yelled, wide-eyed. She pulled me into a room that was half cluttered—half spotless. "I was just in the middle of cleaning." I looked around the room.

The wall by the huge window and the walls across from it were fruit punch red. The other two walls were tan, which made the red pop even more. On one wall stood a dark wooded desk with a bulky computer and a typewriter on it. The other wall had a black vanity and a black book shelf stuck to each end. The book shelves were so cluttered with books that I was surprised not to see any bugs moving around in the dust.

On the wall opposite from the window stood a small couch-like-bed with a bedspread that was the same color as the walls; on it, stood a few pillows either black or zebra print. *I could see myself in a room like this,* I thought. At least she knew how to mix color, unlike that gaudy cabin on the boat. "Yup, this is my room," Witchney said happily, throwing her hands up in the air as if she were displaying the room for a TV show. "So, you're Zaina?" she asked, almost uncertainly.

"Um, yeah?" I said with a baffled look on my face.

"Sorry, it's just I had expected you to be…well, more muscular and beat up," she said, turning the music back on.

"Well, I had imagined you to be—" I began. *Hum*, I thought, *how do I say this nicely?* "taller," I eventually said, causing her to burst into laughter.

"Ha, I get that a lot," she said, not seeming to take much offense to it. "So, I hear we're supposed to save the world," she rolled her eyes. "No pressure or anything," she said while rolling her eyes, causing me to laugh. "How much ya wanna bet this is all just a test?"

"I don't know; everyone's taking this really serious," I said, worriedly. *Well duh*, I thought, *we're talking about the end of the world.*

"Ah, we'll see." she shrugged. "Hey, are you hungry, thirsty or maybe both? I think my mom made her famous mango/coconut shake," she said, happily. I looked at her in confusion. What I really wanted was some aspirin. "You've never had mango or coconut before have you?" she asked, looking at me wide-eyed in astonishment.

"I'm a werewolf. I've never even heard of a shake," I said, almost feeling embarrassed. And it seemed as though she noticed this, too.

"That's okay, I'll show you," she said, giving me a

friendly smile before saying, "And even if you're not thirsty you're gonna try it," she threatened. We both laughed and walked to the kitchen.

Chapter 22

We walked into the kitchen where Phantom and Mrs. Traps had been arguing for quite some time now. Mrs. Traps kept insisting that Witchney wasn't going to go. She said she didn't want her baby to get hurt. I could tell Witchney was embarrassed. Her already rosy cheeks turned target red, making it look like she was wearing too much blush. "But Mrs. Traps! The world depends on Zaina and Witch killing the rebels," Phantom pleaded. Mrs. Traps' head snapped back, giving him a look of disgust.

"I will not allow my little angel to kill anyone!" she yelled angrily. "Even if it means the world. Find someone else. You understand me? Or do I have to get Ellen to teach you a lesson or two?" she said, causing him to cringe.

"Please! I'm just trying to save the world here," he said, a bit too cocky if you ask me.

"No! And that's the end of it," she replied as if she were Phantom's mother too.

He looked over at Witchney. "Can't you try to talk some sense into her?" He seemed so helpless in this situation.

"My mom is a stubborn woman, you know that. The

only person who could ever talk some sense into her is my dad and well… you know where he is." She seemed so suddenly depressed. The way her light seemed to fade sent me a message—a message saying that her father was probably dead or ran away also.

Then Phantom said, "Okay. Well, I guess I'll see you later." Did he really just give up? That was such an anti-Phantom thing to do. He was all about being stubborn and continuously asking a question over and over if he didn't get the answer he wanted. I looked at Witch.

"Tell you later," she whispered. Then we walked over to the fridge.

The shake she served me was absolutely delicious. Though I was a carnivore, that fruit shake was to die for. There was a sweet, tangy flavor coming from the mango, and then there was a soothing after taste from the coconut. No wonder Witchney was so obsessive with Mangos. They were heavenly.

Once we were all done in the kitchen, we returned to her still half cluttered room. "Yeah, sorry about the room being such a mess. Ember said you guys weren't going to get here till the day after tomorrow," she said, picking up a few dirty clothes and throwing them in her closet.   "I'm sorry?" I apologized, not knowing what to say; she just laughed.

"It's fine, really. I guess since it almost the 31st they figured you should get here sooner." She piled a few more books onto the shelf.

"What do you mean?" I asked, my brain not getting a brake from all this new information.

"Ya know, those dreams? When October ends you will be the first to die." She was talking about the diary entries. "Well, there's thirty one days in October and it's the twenty eighth."

"Oh, okay. I know what you're talking about now. Is it really the twenty eighth?" I asked, wondering why they would send us here last minute.

"Yup, the council is crazy. Trust me," she said. Why was everyone asking me to suddenly trust them?

"So, what happened with Phantom back there?" I asked, curiously. She picked up a few more clothes, but this time threw them in a basket.

"Oh, I told him that we would sneak out later. The

world depends on us, right?" she said with the same daredevil smile Phantom always had.

"You told him through thoughts I'm guessing?" I asked, knowing I was right.

"Yeah. Don't you think it's cool how they can do that sort of stuff?" she said. She obviously hadn't been around him that often.

"Actually, I think it's kind of annoying," I said, almost bitterly. She just laughed like she always did.

"Well hey. Look at it this way. If he gets on your nerves too much, just smack him and he'll be all good again," she said, causing us both to laugh. It had never occurred to me to try that tactic.

"So, why does your mom hate him so much?" I asked, hoping I wasn't stepping too far out of my boundaries.

"It's a long story," she said. Before she could continue, her mom called us for lunch.

While Mrs. Traps hated Phantom, she rather liked me. She told me to call her by her first name; Marie. For lunch, we had bell peppers that were stuffed with well-seasoned beef. Again, despite the fact that I was a carnivore, it was delicious.

Some part of me almost seemed to think that Marie knew about our plan to escape. Witchney kept obsessing about how selfish her mother was. She had a point though; her mom didn't want her killing anyone, but if the world spiraled out of control, it wouldn't really matter now would it?

That night, it took Marie forever to finally go to bed. Tonight was the night that her favorite TV show came on. Around midnight, we were finally able to sneak out. Witchney left a note on the fridge that said, "Off to save the world :) Love ya!"

"A bit cocky don't ya think?" I asked, rereading the note.

"Well it's the truth, isn't it?" she asked, rather boastfully. I nodded in semi-agreement.

We both laughed and walked over to the door where Witchney sat down to put on a pair of black converse with pink skull shoe laces. Just then I realized that she had been wearing mixed matched socks the whole time.

"Do you have a pair of shoes I can borrow?" I asked cautiously.

"Do I look like the kind of girl that doesn't have more than one pair of shoes?" she said with a slight attitude. I couldn't really tell if she was being sarcastic or just plain serious. She laughed. "Of course I do. Gosh. You take things too serious!"

After about five minutes, she came back with a pair of neon green converse with neon pink laces. *I won't stand out in a crowd at all,* I thought. She handed me the shoes and a pair of socks—one was blue and pink stripped and the other one black with rainbow colored skulls. "Sorry, I don't have any matching socks," she shrugged. "Quick question; I'm not judging you or anything, but do you even know how to put on shoes?"

"Not really but I can figure it out," I said hopefully, Witchney starting to see my pigheadedness.

"Okay, have fun with that," she said sarcastically, walking into the kitchen once more.

She stood by the door while I fumbled around with the shoes for a while. This was more confusing than I thought it would be. Then out of nowhere, Witchney's phone rang; I might want to add that it was set to full blast. Also, Witch didn't strike me as the type of girl to have 'Love is a Battlefield' as her ring tone.

I heard her mumble something under her breath; she was probably talking to Phantom. Then I heard her say, "What? No, that can't be! But the prophecies," she paused. "Fine, I'll tell Zaina. Bye." She seemed mad. Wonder what that mystery person said.

Ms. Gigi : Around 11:30

I was walking down by the beach, trying to figure out what the prophesies meant. The beach here was lovely. It wasn't like Hollings or Medows. All though, I had to admit that I was a little bewildered at first when I heard that this place was called Blood Lake City. According to the book, this beach was where the witch and the rebel would meet to discuss what would happen next. Yet, as much as I waited and waited, that rebel never showed.

I began to wander. There was some sort of force looming in the air—as if something was trying to get my attention. I kept walking toward this invisible force, eventually stumbling upon my old book of prophesies. *What on earth is it doing here?!* I thought. I examined it, to make sure it was okay. As I looked, I noticed something. It was thinner.

I set the book down immediately and cast a little spell in my head—a spell in hopes to find out what this book really was. As I did so, a set of words formed in my mind. *I am the real book. My twin is a fake.* Frantically, I flipped through the book to try and spot the difference. Then I noticed something; the prophesies about Zaina and Witch were nowhere to be found.

Then I heard a voice from behind me say, "Ha, ha! Fooled ya witch!" I spun around, trying to make sense of it all. Just before the teenage girl could escape, I noticed it was... Well I don't know who it was.

Epilogue

It was frustrating to find out that we weren't supposed to battle the rebels for another two years or so. In the end, it seemed like Witch was the one mad. I just didn't care. I figured that this way I could train more—I'd be more prepared that way I guess.

Ember was in the hospital. At the beach she had called Phantom, after she had found the book. Then she mysteriously blacked out on the phone. He called Witch, hoping she knew what Gigi had been babbling about.

As it turns out, there had never been any prophesies about us fighting the bad guys now—but there were chapters about us and another girl fighting them 'when the bees begin to die.' Whatever that meant. We still didn't know who it was that we were after. But it wasn't Miranda. I could have sworn I was right. Guess not.

In the meantime, I'd joined Witchney at regular school. Today some scientists came in and were talking to us about some genetic experiments they were doing at their labs. Apparently, Bengal Tigers were the only feline survivors after the big storm.

The government wanted to mix the tiger genes and werewolf genes to create a powerful warrior because the government was afraid of something. Of course, they didn't mention who that was. But I did know one thing; I couldn't see this experiment going well.

Author JM Lee

JM Lee is currently a 17 year old author. She started writing *When October Ends* when she was 12, finished it when she was 13, and finally self-published it when she was 14—ironically, at the end of October.

"I don't really know why I like to write," she says during a radio interview, "I guess I like it because it allows me to get away from all the crazy stuff that happens in the world and it allows me to express myself."

The revised edition of book 2, *Chasing,* will be available in January of 2014.

The third and final book of the *Novus Proprius Chronicles*, *Novus Orsa*, will be available summer of 2014.

JM Lee has plans for many more stories—one of which is a steampunk paranormal that takes place in Chicago, 1875, entitled *Blood and Tears*.

For more information visit:
www.novusproprius.com
www.hcspublishing.com

Copyright © 2013 JM Lee

All rights reserved.

ISBN-10: 1493708856

ISBN-13: 978-1493708857

Printed in Poland
by Amazon Fulfillment
Poland Sp. z o.o., Wrocław